Secret Breakfast

twenty-eight fresh fables

Secret Breakfast: twenty-eight fresh fables

by Candace Leigh Coulombe

ISBN: 978-1456340148

www.secretbreakfast.com

Recognition for Candace Leigh Coulombe's stories:

Several *Secret Breakfast* stories were originally published in *Second Grace*, which was the Compilations/Anthologies Winner in the 2010 Beach Book Festival and received an Honorable Mention in the 2010 San Francisco Book Festival. *Second Grace* was also recognized by *The Sacramento Book Review* and the podcast series *Audible Authors*.

"ScentEasy" received the 2009 Environmental Futures Writing Prize at the National League of American PEN Women Soul-Making Literary Awards. "Duck, Duck, Goose" received an Honorable Mention in the Mary Kennedy Eastman Flash Fiction Prize in the 2010 Soul-Making Awards.

"The Changing Room" received an award in Sacramento Public Library's Focus on Writers Competition in 2009 and an award in the 15th Dame Lisbet Throckmorton Fiction Writing Contest in 2010.

Elk Grove Public Library presented awards to "The Voracious Reader" in 2009 and to "Fruit of the Spirit" in 2010.

"Cold Call" received an Honorable Mention in NYC Midnight Short Story Competition in 2008. "Cleanliness Is" placed in NYC Midnight Creative Writing Championship in 2009.

An abridged version of "My Better Nature" was a First and Second Round Finalist in Reading Writer's "Snow" Flash Fiction Contest.

"A Noise that Doesn't Stop" was originally published in the Insomnia Issue of *Wilde-Paris*.

"The Gulf of Aden" was originally published on CellStories.

- TABLE OF CONTENTS -

Fables Fantastic

Fables Domestic

RESOURCES FOR READERS

Fables Fantastic

Absinthe Minded

*A woodland police station gets mired
in the misadventures of green fairies.*

These sort of days aggravated Constable Bell's dyspepsia. The blooming season brought its annual onslaught of property disputes and lovers' quarrels to the station. But the Fées Vertes brought, well, more urban problems to the Bois Blanc precinct.

Over the past few years, Canterbury Bell had witnessed more human writers, uninspired by their city surroundings, venturing wide-eyed to the woods. And with more artists comes a certain kind of fairy. Frankly, a fairy tough for even Bell to tame. The Fées Vertes showed little respect for woodland conventions. They played wild and late, dressed in little more than wisps of fog, and mercilessly teased the local boys. In fact, the same talent to which gave muse to artists and authors also seduced imps, elves, and sprites. As well as other creatures. Things always ended badly—the defenestration of adversaries, rent petals, and tears. And the Vertes, capricious by nature, would tire of the attentions of their new plaything and seek the protection of Bell's office from stalking. This is how the rule of law came to be.

The Bois Blanc station, adeptly run by Constable Canterbury Bell, simply did not have the bandwidth to handle other creature crimes. Even if an elfin boy was found to be overly rough with a fairy paramour, it was tough to tell what kind of magic would keep him in his cell. And if a troll or goblin, or (heaven's sake) a squirrel, were charged, the fairy station could not hold him. It wasn't miscegenation, just practicality. The station at its tallest point was five inches-three. So, Kingcup Fairy and Queen-of-the-Meadow ordered a rule be established outside the door. A human measuring-stick was enchanted and planted in the ground. Creatures more than four inches tall could not be detained, merely banished from the fairy ring. While this kept Bell's cells free for fairy perpetrators, it encouraged the mischievous Vertes to make many and more claims. Once tired of certain affection, or annoyed by a pretty garden-variety rival, the Vertes sought quick dispatch.

Though he realized that often they were truly in trouble, Bell had little sympathy for the Vertes. This day, he was settling a dispute between the unrelated fairies of Greater and Lesser Celandine, and investigating the mysterious vandalism of the Strawberry Festival pavilion. So, when lovely Fanchon swept in seeking assistance, he made her sit and wait.

Fanchon's disheveled state only emphasized the sultry beauty which caused the gossip of her neighbors. Her hair was mussed, her cheeks ruddy, the shredded tips of her wings tangled on the breeze. The smell of Florence fennel filled the little office as each tear fell. And between the whimpers, Bell noted her once-euphonic tinkle had an off-note, like toy piano out-of-tune.

"Fanchon Artemisia, what kind have trouble have you gotten yourself into today?" bellowed Bell.

"Oh, Canterbury…"

"That's Constable Bell."

"Oh, Canterbury, I've had the most terrible fortune. I need your help!"

"Who is it this time, Fanchon? An angry gnome?"

As a flower-fairy himself, Bell was as rather hurt and offended that he was regarded too foppish for a Verte. But even he could see that her wings had been manhandled. She wore one lonely little green shoe.

"For whatever personal reasons you do not care for me," Fanchon held, "I have just as much right to report a crime as any fairy… and to be treated fairly."

Fanchon slipped off her shoe and set in gingerly in her lap. She crossed her bare ankles and began her tale.

"I am quite good at what I do, you know. We sisters don't grow pansies. We grow flowers in the minds of men. Art, music, prose, and rhyme is Fées' work. Fiction is my specialty.

I came to a writer's cottage this very June. And in it I found a man of such considerable skill, I was taxed to assist him. I could only share my secrets to better content. The talent was all his. Still, he treated me with much gratitude and affection. It was difficult not to express my... esteem.

The writer made me a seat on the finest crystal cup and silver spoon. I would sit and encourage his work deep into the night. He, in turn, would feed me sugar cubes and cool water. One evening, enamored by our success, I kissed him. I kissed him, Canterbury, right on the mouth!"

Bell felt his cheeks flush with envy. "And then?"

"Then the man's wife came into the study," Fanchon said quietly. "She called me a moral disgrace. She said I was a vice... "

"Cruel, yes, Fanchon, but not a crime."

"She put some cotton wool close to my face, and I lost time. But when I woke, two pushpins speared my wings. I was tethered to a white board next to deceased *Lycaena mariposa*. It was after much sacrifice I was able to fashion my escape.... I can no longer fly... "

The constable melted a bit. "I don't know what justice I can offer. You know the rule of law."

"That's all I request."

A dark shadow descended over the station. Bell opened the doors to reveal the unfortunately familiar view of a man's loafer. The writer towered almost six feet over the ruler. He bent awkwardly to retrieve it, having recognized it as missing from his own desk drawer. A leather elbow patch brushed the station, quaking the inhabitants. And just as the writer shook soil from the ruler, a great explosion catapulted him across the wood. Befuddled by the blast, the man strode forward. He smacked comically into nothing, as a sparrow colliding with an overly-clean window. Try as he might, he could not pass into the fairy ring.

"Thank you, Canterbury." Fanchon kissed the constable on the cheek.

"But your wings, your lovely wings," Bell shook his head.

"I have no power for flight," she conceded. "But he has no book." Fanchon smiled. "The manuscript for *The Complete Book of Fairies* lies safely within the ring."

Buses and Planes

As a centenarian waits at his bus stop, a memorable and menacing man weaves a true tale of a crime gone wrong.

Isidor Fisch doesn't like company at the bus stop. Most days, he waits alone. Some mornings little old ladies sit and knit on the bench, then, remembering they don't need the bus after all, pack up their skeins and go. Isidor Fisch is 103, but he knows an old lady when he sees one. Some mornings, Isidor gets tired of waiting and wheels himself back home.

Having seen a century, he's in pretty good shape. He navigates the grounds in his chair, legs atrophied but arms strong. A fur blanket covers his lap on cool days and fair. He doesn't remember what he ate for breakfast, but he does remember the seam on Gerta's stockings in 1932. And, for the record, tuberculosis didn't get the better of him back in '34.

Today, a stranger wipes his boots on the edge of the bench. The smell of fertilizer and mashed May heliotrope reminds Isidor of a garden in Hopewell. A garden he set foot in once only, seventy-five years ago.

The stranger is both strange and familiar. At least he thinks he's a stranger. Memory itself can be strange. The stranger is dressed as a gentleman should: suit, tie, and hat, all well-cut if a bit burnt around the seams. He's younger than Isidor by generations.

"Mind if I smoke, Mr. Fisch?"

The old man bends his head in apathy. The young man produces a sterling case from his jacket pocket. The initials *BRH* glint in the sun. The young man slips a brown cigarette into his mouth and takes a deep drag. The tip crackles and glows orange, no lighter required. The old man considers this a moment, but resolves that he's seen many strange things lately. Perhaps some things only make sense in the minds of the young.

Circles of smoke rest in the air between them. First black, then red, then blue.

"We may have a bit of a wait," offers Isidor. "This bus is often late."

"I have time… and a story," replies the young man.

A breeze whips around Isidor's wheelchair, ringing like children's church hand bells. He pulls his blanket in tight. What cheek, thinks the old man. I've seen and done things this kid couldn't conceive. What story could entertain me?

"I know you're fond of stories," prods the young man. "In fact, Fisch story was coined after you."

"Do I know you?" Isidor whispers.

Without wince or whimper, the young man stamps the cigarette out on a faded eaglet tattoo on the back of his wrist. He tosses the butt on the ground and sticks out his hand.

"I'm Bruno. From Queens by way of Old Smokey."

The old man reluctantly meets his handshake. A jolt of static runs up through his arm, out his elbow, connects to the chair, and rebounds through his arm again. A black mark blooms on Isidor's hand.

"You know the story, Mr. Fisch. You may even know how it ends. But, you don't know how it feels… It's the story of the century."

The old man tries vainly to manipulate his chair. The wheels did not budge. He musters his composure before looking Bruno in the eye.

"I don't remember."

"You will."

Bruno stretches his arms theatrically, cracking his knuckles over his head. He then settles himself comfortably on the bench.

"We'll start in the middle, I think. Let's see… When I finally was able to come to America, things were still very hard. Not as hard as what I suffered in the war, you understand, nor prison in Bautzen, but my wife Anna and I were very poor. And, I am ashamed to admit, I committed a few petty crimes to keep us in our flat."

Isidor wonders which war Bruno means, but sits silent.

"My associate, a furrier known for making good money with supplementary schemes, asked me to invest seventy-five hundred dollars. Now this was no small means to accomplish, but my associate promised hundreds of thousands of dollars in return. Time passed, and I worried that I had made a foolish investment, but I did not want to question a successful and, candidly, dangerous man. The associate asked me to keep a box safe in my home while he took a short trip. I assumed the best for my investment, reasoning I had some type of confidential collateral. Until very recently, I did not see this man again.

"Every day my wife hung her apron on a hook above the shelf where the box sat. Four months later, I read in the paper that this associate had succumbed to a disease. I opened the box, Mr. Fisch, and do you know what it contained?"

"Perhaps," utters the old man.

"Forty thousand dollars in gold certificates," the young man says with a smile. "Well, those certificates were then in the process of being taken out of circulation, so claiming them for myself, I quickly took advantage of the return of my investment. I bought a dark blue Dodge sedan. And do you know what happened next?"

The two men regard each other intently. To Isidor, Bruno appears to be thirty or so, certainly no older than thirty-five.

"I thought you were dead," hisses the old man.

Bruno laughs. "I thought you were dead, too."

Bruno takes another cigarette from his case. Again it magically lights, unaided by match.

"Now that we have the pleasantries over with," he puffs, "I can continue our tale... Next, Mr. Fisch,—that is, Isidor,—one of the spent gold certificates was traced back to me. I wasn't surprised to learn that the funds were ill-gotten. But, I must admit, I was not prepared to find that my new fortune came from the most infamous kidnapping case in the world."

Bruno exhales. A noxious smoke cloud hits the roof of the bus shelter and disperses. The air smells of celery, olives, chicken, potato fries, buttered peas, cherries, and cake.

"Last supper," Bruno apologizes. "It lingers." He blows a red ring of smoke.

"Even if you can't remember your last meal, Isidor, you'll remember the crime. A cherub-faced toddler, darling to his parents, who themselves were the darlings of America, was taken from the nursery in the dark of the night. His father met the kidnapper's ransom, but the boy was not returned. Ah, I see you're feeling the story now."

The old man's face, in fact, is feeling a bit warm. His wrinkles began to fade and his cheeks grow plump and rosy. His bare pate stings as golden curls begin springing through his scalp. Pearly kernels of baby teeth begin cutting through. His gums, only accustomed to rice pudding and creamed corn, swell and flush with ache. He clutches his blanket in dread and confusion, but instead of fur, he feels only thick flannel.

"It was months before the toddler's body was discovered," continues Bruno. "And what a state! So bad, the investigators couldn't tell at first whether it was a boy or girl. I think that he was identified by the overlapping toes on the right foot. It must have been the right, because the left leg…"

"Stop! Stop!" screams the old man. "It was too long ago. I'm a different man…"

Bruno doesn't flinch. "Yet, I am the same. So, we continue. It must have been the right foot, because the left leg was missing."

Isidor's right leg twitches as his middle toe curls and shrivels up to the shape of a petrified seahorse. His left leg, which had been spared from sensation for many years, begins to shake under the blanket. There is a rending noise as the tendons and muscles separate against the grain. A sharp crack as the thighbone snaps. A sickly slithering, like fingers combing through hot cheese casserole, and a metallic thump like the casserole dish falling downstairs. His left leg bangs against the footrest of the wheelchair. Then, just as suddenly, it is gone.

"Please stop!" he screams again.

Bruno calmly speaks on. "And both hands were missing."

The old man flails, his face contorts in pain. The blanket slips from his grasp. His palms open, as if in a gesture of acceptance, but an unseen pressure on his thumbs keeps turning his wrists one full circle and then another. The bones in his wrists make a tinfoil crackle. His hands bend at unnatural angles. They twist and twist until they simply pop off. Explode, really—two gory Christmas crackers throwing blood and bits of bone instead of confetti.

"I'll wait to tell you how he met his unfortunate end until after I tell you how I met mine."

The creature in the wheelchair pants and weeps from temporary relief. He now has pudgy cheeks of a baby, blonde curls, blue eyes, one leg, no hands, and infinite fear.

"They had eight experts testify that my handwriting matched that on the demand note. They matched wood from my garage to the grain of the ladder used for the crime. And, I had those damned gold certificates which had been paid as ransom.

"No fingerprints, Isidor. No evidence except circumstantial. No motive to hurt anybody's baby. I was no angel, but I never would have hurt a kid. Even the governor vouched for me.

"They fried me up at New Jersey State. That should've been you."

The old man braces his body for an electric shock, but no jolt comes.

"Imagine this little boy, just old enough to know the words *mama* and *daddy*, scared, cold, and hurting. Taken from his warm bed to a rickety old boat in the middle of the night. Bludgeoned to death and dumped in a field four miles from home."

The old man feels something warm and sticky seep through his new curls. A gash opens in the back of his head. It grows deeper and wider, oozing blood and greenish syrup. Isidor can taste his own brain fluid in the back of his throat.

"We dropped him from the ladder," he cries. "It was an accident. An accident! We just wanted the money. But the package was dead before we even delivered the note. I remember now. It was an accident!"

"He wasn't even two." Bruno betrays no emotion. "He never had a chance to do anything but good. In two lifetimes, you and I put together couldn't come up with two years of good."

The old man's bloody blonde head rolls forward against his chest. Bruno speaks once more, though he knows he is no longer heard. "The little body was badly decomposed."

Heliotrope sprouts from the discarded cigarette. Isidor's body turns from pink to black to green and then succumbs to the blooms. Little purple blossoms twist through the spokes of the wheelchair, covering the decay with their cherry pie scent. Bruno snaps a few and places them decorously in his buttonhole. He sits, waits, and is rewarded with the arrival of his bus: Number 35, Fresh Pond Crematory Line.

As he boards the bus, a woman in white runs toward him

across the green.

"Wait!" she shouts. "This isn't a bus stop!"

"A bus stopped for me, miss. You must be mistaken."

Number 35 pulls away from the curb and vanishes down the lane. The woman's companion waits for an explanation. She smoothes her skirt and straightens her cap.

"As I was saying, we have many amenities here for people with your father's challenges. We find it's best to accommodate their delusions—only harmless ones, of course. And, well, those with dementia often feel the need to go take care of a task, to leave the facility."

"I don't quite follow you, Nurse Anne."

"We erected this fake bus shelter in the garden a few years ago. It gives our older residents a destination. People with dementia can be very restless. They're contented with the idea that a bus will come to take them where they need to go. After a few minutes or a few hours, they'll have forgotten why they were waiting for a bus in the first place. It seems to be soothing for them."

A white-haired lady pardons herself past them and perches her knitting bag on the bench.

"Where are you headed today?" the nurse gently asks.

"Home," she says with worry. "I think I left the oven on."

"Well, come on back if you remember otherwise, dear."

The nurse leans over to pick up a spent butt, and spots something blue under the heliotrope. It's a baby blanket of the softest flannel. It is spattered with little airplanes and little stars.

What a strange day, she thinks. Buses, no buses, babies, and planes. Perhaps some things only make sense in the minds of the old.

Cleanliness Is

A repentant Thunderbird is redeemed by a divine car wash.

The Thunderbird idled at the stop, unsure of which direction to pursue. Hand wash or In-Bay Automatic? The SUV behind him honked, and he turned left toward the IBA. It had been so long, and he was so self-conscious as it was, that he'd rather not opt for face-to-face.

He queued up behind the other dirty cars. As he waited, he examined his conscience. When the light indicated the wash was free, he eased onto the track until the tire sensor blinked.

"Welcome," intoned the automated attendant. "Relax into neutral, release all brakes, and refrain from steering."

The T-Bird shuddered under the rollers. He felt queasy.

"Bless me in this car wash. It has been almost one year since my last cleanse.... "

"Go on, my child."

The ribbon-like curtains of the mitter fluttered side to side in the bay as the T-Bird exhaled. He started with the venial sins.

"I accuse myself of speeding, of speeding in a school zone.... I've been indulging too much, too often in high-octane fuel lately and..."

"Yes?"

"And, I can be prideful. I think I let the J.D. Power Best in Class award go to my head.... Car of the Year from Motor Trend, too."

"Back in 2002?"

"Yeah," whispered the roadster. "My father was loved since he rolled out of the Dearborn plant. I don't know, maybe I'm not a classic like him. Maybe I'm just a throwback."

"You are loved. Your Father knows you by VIN number. He knows your weaknesses and your talents," advised the attendant. "You have a top-shift, fully-synchronized, five-speed manual transmission. I encourage you to reflect on your life. Pray for humility, simplicity, and joy in fifth."

"I will. I'll try. It's just, there's something else...." The T-Bird entered the high-pressure rinse stage. "It was an accident, really it was. I mean, I had my stereo up, my windows down, and I was really cruising along. I couldn't stop in time. I didn't stop at all...."

He leaked a little washer fluid as he confessed. "I killed a cat today. There was a ginger streak—so fast—and then I felt her limp body thump under my tires."

The nozzles aimed at his wheels, removing brake dust and build-up. Closed-cell foam wraparounds rubbed his front bumper, washed his sides, and then worked along his license plate area. Rocker panel washers cleaned away the remnants of fur, the smatter of blood.

The attendant counseled the T-Bird and, with great care, assigned his penance.

"Do not despair of Ford's mercy," said the attendant. "The Maker has reconciled the world to Himself and sent the Mechanic among us for the forgiveness of sins. You have a contrite heart, and you have His pardon and peace. You are absolved."

Pink, blue, and yellow triple foamers cleansed the roadster and coated him with protective paint sealant. The spot-free water and forced air dried him immaculately. He exited the bay clean and with purpose.

The T-Bird retraced his morning route until he came to the unfortunate place. He pulled off on the gravel shoulder, but kept his engine running. He popped open his passenger-side door.

"Hello? Is there anyone there?" he asked gently.

A weak meow replied. A chorus of mewing followed. A trio of lonely, confused kittens rolled over each other. His chrome was slippery against their paws. Eventually, they were able to clamber from the wheel well to the floor. Their tiny claws more tickled than scratched his upholstery as they scaled the seat. The sun streamed through the little porthole window, breaking a rainbow across their soft orange backs. They cuddled each other for comfort and purred.

Ford, you know all things, the Thunderbird prayed. *You know that I love you.*

Cold Call

An optimistic cosmetics saleslady pays a call on a spectral customer. Perhaps they each have just what the other needs.

Daisy Jameson will be an Independent Senior Director this year. In fact, she's telling herself now.

"I, Daisy J. Jameson, will join the Circle of Achievement this year," she says to the review mirror. "I am empowered to realize my dream of career success." She reapplies her Sassy Pink Fabulous Lip Color and checks her teeth for cupcake frosting. The car behind her honks irritably and she proceeds through the intersection.

It's hot. Her new skirt-suit, in the same shade of Sassy Pink, is pure polyester. She cracks the Accord's window, but not enough to mess her hair. She parks in a shaded side street and pops the hatchback. Once she recruits twelve consultants and meets her sales goals, she'll be eligible for a brand new Mustang. And if she becomes a Senior Executive Director, maybe even a Mercedes. Then she'd be proud to park in front of any customer's, that is client's, home.

Now, however, she gently pats away a little moustache of sweat and wishes for A/C. Hopefully, her beauty case has stayed cool. How embarrassing it would be to pop open her portable candy store of cosmetics, only to show pink pools of melted wax.

Daisy repeats her personal affirmation. Her thighs are audible as they brush together, sausaged into drugstore stockings.

Shish-shush with every step. The buttons of her jacket strain to stay in their buttonholes. Perhaps she's put a little on since Dale's been gone. She still has a pretty face and a personality to match. At least, that's what the Senior Executive Director leading the two-day Beauty University said. So Daisy wrote her a check for $500, and set out with conviction and a fresh case of product samples.

That was Thursday. By the weekend, Daisy had set out 24 slotted cardboard boxes, pads and pens in friendly shops around town. "Become Your Best Self – FREE Skincare & Cosmetic Consultations" touted the boxes. But on Wednesday, as she dutifully shook each for leads, mostly candy wrappers fell out. From some boxes, worse.

At the diner, her last stop, she felt an acute pang of doubt. A pink and green buttercream cupcake and a Tab settled her stomach. "Five-hundred dollars," she sighed, "five-oh-oh."

As she counted her change, the waitress slid the cardboard box down the counter. "Don't forget this, honey."

A folded note stuck half-in half-out of the slot. Under "Call me today to schedule my complimentary, no-obligation professional consultation!" there was no phone number, simply "2932 Lily Parkway" and "Thank you. Beryl."

Daisy clicks down Lily Parkway in Sassy Pink heels. She finds 2930 and 2934 and marches to the door of the house between. She repeats her affirmation once more before ringing the bell.

Silence.

Daisy pushes the button again. A little jolt of electricity arcs to her finger. Zot! The button blackens. Just burns out.

She blows out the smoldering tip of one acrylic nail. "Beauty calling... Anyone home?"

The door creaks open, cutting a swath in the dusty foyer floor. "Come in," she hears. "I've been expecting you."

Daisy follows the voice down the hall to a study. Narrow ribbons of sunlight eke between the closed shutters. They trip across a sterling letter opener, a crystal paperweight, an engraved snuffbox, and the gilded bindings of several books strewn across the room. Daisy blows the dust off two covers and discovers *West with the Night* and *The Splendid Outcast*. She sets them on the desk next to a book by Saint Exupèry – a name she remembers from her childhood. A book about a little boy on a lonely little planet. A little boy and a rose.

I am in the wrong place, she thinks. And just as fast she

corrects herself. Every interaction is an opportunity to share the life-changing benefits of True Beauty. "Beryl? Is there a Beryl here?"

"Yes, that's me. I've been waiting for you."

Daisy looks doubtfully at the neglected study. Every woman deserves and can afford beauty she remembers from her training. She regains her Sassy Pink smile.

There is a shuffle of slippers and Beryl appears. She is cocooned in a man's cable-knit cardigan with suede elbow patches. It smells as if tobacco and honeysuckle are stashed in her pockets. Daisy realizes she was expecting an old woman. An old woman in a dusty study, with an old name like Beryl, lonely and looking for company instead of lipstick. She looks barely twenty. Just a girl, really.

"Welcome," she says and extends a pale cool hand.

Beauty University taught a three-point selling system: One, meet the client's immediate need. Two, get them into a core daily-use product. And then, three, match them with something special specific to their lifestyle.

Temperature I can't do too much about, Daisy thinks. "You have such a pretty face. Have you ever tried a bronzer?"

"Oh, do make yourself comfortable." Daisy hears the cheerful clink of ice cubes. Beryl motions to two cut-crystal tumblers brimming with something sparkling pink and garnished with mint. "I've had hardly any company since Papa died. And none at all since the crash."

The word crash lingers in the air between them. Daisy finally breaks the silence with the sharp clack of the clasps on her case. She motions toward the cracked leather wingchair.

"Oh, do make *your*self comfortable," Daisy counters. "I'll get started. Just relax, chat if you'd like."

"Well, okay… "

As Beryl sits, she brushes the chair's arm and the brass nailhead trim oxidizes a bright blue-green under her fingers.

"Tell me about your current skincare routine… "

"I don't really, I mean, I guess it was just soap and water." Daisy smiles at her reassuringly. "I never much cared about this sort of thing. But lately… oh, I thought a change might help. Perhaps they were right."

"They who?"

"My family. My mother and sisters were very ladylike. They were attentive to their beauty."

"You have such a pretty face, too," Daisy repeats with a smile. But pretty wasn't quite the right word. Though her eyes take on the lucid green of a cut gem, Beryl's face is drawn and pale. Daisy can feel its chill through the cotton pad of ph-balanced astringent. With each touch, Beryl's skin takes on progressive translucency.

"Perhaps some color?" offers Daisy. "We could play up your emerald eyes with an aquamarine shadow. Lip gloss? What do you like? I'm thinking Morganite Pink, Scarlet Siren, or Riesling Red."

"Oh, you choose."

The lip gloss has a similar strange effect. It shimmers at first and then dissipates, taking more of Beryl's scarce natural color with it. Daisy looks helplessly at the row of candy-colored compacts. She takes a drink of the sparkling concoction.

They didn't cover this in training.

"Tell me a bit about yourself," she stalls. "We have so many wonderful True Beauty products, I want to be sure and show you what meets your needs. What do you like?"

Beryl thinks for a moment. "I like green."

"Well, that's a good start."

"I liked gardens, topiary, hedges, and hedgehogs. I liked flowerbeds and fat velvet honeybees. I liked croquet on the lawn." Her cheeks briefly flush pink.

"I liked my Papa. The smell of his pipe in this study. The crinkle of pages as he read the Sunday news. I liked flying with him best off all."

It's hard to lose a good man, thinks Daisy. There's so few to go around. There's so few it's hard to lose a bad one, too.

"He really was a good man," Beryl says aloud. "I don't mean to compare fathers with husbands. That's a different loss.... " Daisy cautiously takes another drink.

"But Papa... He shared his library with me. We went to the horse races together. Oh, how my mother hated that! And he even let me fly his plane... " The color drains from her cheeks just as quickly as it had come. "It seems as though I've lost the capacity for flight."

Daisy rummages through the case. "I think," she says finally, "I have just the thing."

She presents a fancy topaz atomizer. "It's new. It's only for those women ready for True Beauty. Ready to invest in the preservation of beauty." "Inside and out," she adds, so as not to sound shallow. "It's called Sweet Repose."

Daisy squeezes the gold bulb and spritzes the air. There's a ting-ting-ting like a triangle being played in grade school band. "We've had Sweet Rose and Sweet Vanilla sprays for a while, but this is special."

Beryl tries the atomizer herself. A bright spark flashes as each droplet touches her skin. "I had a good feeling about you," says Beryl. "Your check is on the tray, Daisy J. Jameson."

"I don't understand... "

Spritz! Spark, spark, spark! Beryl keeps dousing herself in Sweet Repose. "The paperweight, it's crystal, you see. Beryl mineral, actually. It's for scrying. We've had it in the family for years."

"It's for crying?"

"No, no, scrying." Beryl is sparking more now. "Scrying,

seeing the future. So happiness sometimes, I guess, and crying others."

Bits of light shine where bits of Beryl used to be. "I won't have much use for it now." The ball falls through her sparking fingers and rolls out of the study. "Follow it, Daisy J. Jameson, if you want to know your fate."

Beryl lights up like a chandelier. The bottle of Sweet Repose of the Soul falls indecorously to the floor. Daisy folds the $500 check into her polyester pocket and runs awkwardly in her pink pumps after the scrying crystal. It rolls down the hall and bumps down the steps. It keeps rolling down the sidewalk of Lily Parkway.

The house goes very bright and then –pop- it's out like a burnt bulb. It's gone. There's a honeysuckle hedge rich with bees where 2932 should be.

Daisy turns her attention back to the accelerating ball. A man unloads bakery boxes from a white delivery truck and turns to cross its path. The ball hits the side of his handcart with surprising force. It sounds as if a thousand triangles have simultaneously been dropped on the sidewalk.

"No!" Daisy shouts. She collapses right there on the curb, not even caring to sit like a lady. The man kneels down and offers her the sleeve of his white jacket.

"I don't have a handkerchief," he apologizes. Daisy wipes the mascara racooning under her eyes with her finger. She wipes her black finger on his sleeve.

"There you go," he laughs.

He's handsome. More than Dale was even.

"You look too pretty in pink to be so upset," he says. He reaches for the top box off the cart. "Would you like a cupcake?"

Emergency Sirens

*A baby abandoned at a bus stop is pacified
with otherworldly intercession.*

Had it been another time, another town, it would have been a changeling story. In fables, the inconsolable babe is left in the woods so that the faeries may reclaim her and replace her with the human they'd earlier switched. In fact, it was not too many years ago that a developmentally disabled child would be so abandoned with hopes from the mother of the return of her rightful human one. Had it been someplace greener, Essex or Cornwall, there might be faeries or pixies or sprites. But it was not. It was that unfortunate kind of area neither urban enough to be cultured nor suburban enough to be safe. And the only time it was remotely clean was the fifteen minutes after a rainstorm.

And the baby left in a Moses basket on the wet bench of the bus stop was not a faerie. Her crying was not the result of misadaptation to human life, but simply the appropriate response to neglect and all-too-human disappointment. Her mother had boarded #17, railway station-bound, on its last run of the night. In desperation, one will try anything, and in hopelessness, nothing at all. The mother leaving the unfortunate baby and the unfortunate town had never learned how to live in the world. A baby was beyond her diminishing capacity. And, in her brokenness, she did not consider the fate of the precious parcel left behind. She had given her life, fair hair and dark eyes, a wool flannel blanket, a soother – and that was all.

The streets were still wet. The night air was cool and fresh on the baby's cheeks. She cooed as the stoplights flashed green then yellow then red, their puddle reflections blinking the same. The traffic on the cross streets sounded like rolling waves. About ten minutes passed without anxiety. And then, sirens broke through the night. They echoed down the avenue, so loud as to be mythic. The noise was a regular occurrence in the neighborhood, but new to the little one. She commenced a terrible wail of her own. The plastic soother fell unceremoniously onto the pavement.

The baby's distress rivaled that of the emergency sirens. Perhaps this is how she came to the attention of three local girls that night.

Ondine, Lorelei, and Morgan were grunge-like disheveled in dress, though all distractingly pretty beneath long locks still glistening from the rain. Lorelei swept a snarled curl off her face and examined the crier more closely.

"Is she alone?"

The others surveyed the dark street and shrugged. Morgan poked the baby with her finger.

"She's real."

The poking didn't help matters. The baby wailed harder. Morgan spied the soother and regarded the grit on its rubber nipple.

"No," Ondine chided. "That's gross."

"Well, we have to do something to pacify her…"

Ondine pulled off her fisherman's sweater, lifted the baby from the basket, and wrapped her up. The baby nuzzled against a cabled sleeve and blinked her wet lashes at Ondine.

The girls gathered together to form a shelter around the child. They conferred in a whisper and then began to softly sing. A few cars sped down the dark street, their drivers unaware. Once they'd passed, the song bloomed full and clear. Their voices were replete with lightness, lilt, and beauty. The music was intoxicating. And, had anyone else heard that night, they would have quite literally been driven to distraction. The voices were none but the girls' own. The lyrics, however, were W.H. Auden's:

> *Let the winds of dawn that blow*
> *Softly round your dreaming head*
> *Such a day of sweetness show*
> *Eye and knocking heart may bless,*
> *Find the mortal world enough;*

Noons of dryness see you fed
by the involuntary powers,
Nights of insult let you pass
Watched by every human love.

The baby gurgled happily. She was lit momentarily by passing headlamps, and the girls saw her English-rose face in its prettiness for the first time. Near-white curls showed from beneath her knit cap. Even in the dim light, they could see her eyes were the deep color of brambleberries. For a baby who was motherless, thirsty, and a bit damp, she was just lovely.

The girls exchanged knowing glances.

"She's looks just like Nixie," Lorelei said at last.

They nodded. Nix hadn't been seen or spoken of for dozens of their years. Her eyes, though, were an indelible shade of indigo. Nix had been trouble: a caterwauling baby, a reckless girl, and a teenager unreined. Nix had a softness for men and made terrible decisions for their favor. She had, to their relief, left to make her own way.

And here was this wee thing, so like Nix in coloring, but pink and new. Filled with the promise of, well, everything.

The baby was as plump as a seal pup, but showed the beauty of Circe in her color and little rosebud of a mouth. Ondine sang a little tune, and the baby brightened and cooed.

The girls conferred again. All three put their hands in to cradle the child. And, with a shake of their skirts and stamp of boots, the four disappeared in the sparkling night.

Once they had vanished, the clouds opened again. The storm upturned the empty basket. A flurry of opalescent feathers and scales was washed from the bus stop before the morning route even began.

Endure, Adapt, Overcome

A man with a special gift for survival returns to the site of his remote shelter to complete its construction.

They had been building it to withstand anything, but James was surprised to see it standing at all. It, though interrupted, stood in grey Euclidean planes against the bright green of Appalachia. Five years later, the walls stood ready to be proofed in Kevlar, the water reservoir full and ready to be filtered. The Faraday cage glinted copper, empty and clean as a new coop awaiting its first hens and eggs.

The thing about a survival shelter is that it has to be complete to be of any help.

The construction had been a matter of debate between James and Sabine. She had wanted a cabin, a place to raise goats, grow her own vegetables, that sort of thing. And he, well, he wanted barracks. But, even with his skills, it was tough to erect a structure that can withstand nuclear fallout without the proper tools. Perhaps she was right. At least, a pregnant woman wanting to live sustainably doesn't attract the same kind of consternation as a conspiracy nut. If he actually was one, it only made it worse to have all those workers and suppliers trucking up the hill.

It turned out they both were wrong. At least, they were overly optimistic for survivalists.

For most of his life, James had been considered a lucky man. And, in marrying Sabine, blessed. He emerged unscathed from atrocious accidents. In a life of near-misses, almost perfectly scar-free, she was the only thing that had hit its mark. When they took her, when they took her… it had done exactly what they wanted: it weaponized him.

In his youth, his luck was unbroken. When an air hammer misfired, the industrial nail left only the slightest dimple above his brow. When he fell from his dorm window in a night of co-ed revelry, he only suffered from grass stains. And when his flight, in a botched hijacking attempt, crashed in an Iowan cornfield, James walked out through the flaming husks barely singed.

After that, he knew it was more than luck. Whatever this gift was, he had tried to use it for good. There are many enemies to be made in pursuit of such. There are many ways to test indestructibility.

They had started building the structure after Sabine told him about the baby. At first, it was to be a place where they could have a sense of normalcy. A place immune from the publicity and demands of his specialized kind of community service. And then, as his list of adversaries grew, it was to become a place to protect his family. As his resilience grew, so did his confidence. His immunity to injury seemed to be approaching immortality. And, after a little while, it seemed that the safe house wouldn't be needed. He thought he could keep them safe anywhere.

Now, here he was, alone. Though the site was an isolated area, he still waited until nightfall to amble the truck down the hill and scavenge for supplies. He made do. James filled the walls with sand and gravel to slow ballistics. He wasn't afraid of getting shot, only of a hole in the wall which they could pull him through. There wasn't much time left. Sure, he'd done a share of hero work, but he wasn't like them. He didn't have training in combat or espionage. He just had a body that was its own shield. They thought it could be even more.

They tried to replicate and amplify his ability. In certain situations, they learned, his body could not only withstand trauma, but also return it. They tested Sabine. They tested the baby. And neither had the same gift as James.

In good moments now, he planned for root vegetables, laundry lines, and goats. In bad ones, most moments, he sat on the floor of the Faraday cage. Protected from EMP and RF, shielded from their frequencies by the copper mesh, James attempted to remove the tracking chip from his heel. The more he tried to slice it out, to sever their trace, the more his body rebelled.

The thing about a fierce survival gene is that it won't allow you to cut yourself.

They were coming to take him. And, with his luck, he could only ever be taken alive.

Fruit of the Spirit

Three sisters are too good for the liking of their neighbors.

We do not like them. There are three sisters, Agatha, Catherine, and Lucy, and we dislike them equally. They came last spring almost at the end of the semester. At Friday mass, they each genuflected before the Host. One fluid movement, a piece of dance that didn't seem possible: right knee, left knee, sign of the cross, mouth opens gently, left foot, right foot, back quietly to the pew. They knelt there until the proper moment, after the tabernacle was closed again. We could only see the dove-colored ribbons streaming down their backs in hair that had seen a hundred brushstrokes before bedtime.

They had taken down the hems of their skirts. There was a faint ridge in the wool where they'd used a seam ripper, and neat new series of green stitches against the plaid. Their pleats hit the bottom of the knee. Our waistbands were rolled up until it was almost indecent to use the kneeler. They wore soft silk blouses with pearl buttons, like our mother's, and we had hand-me-downs from our brother's uniform. Our shirts buttoned on the wrong side.

In the summer, we were relieved to t-shirts of concerts never seen and cut-off dungarees. We smoked to distraction, ate little and drank much, listened to records, fought and reconciled. We never saw their mother either. They surely had one. When we looked through the fence slats, they were always there. Though we heard laughter, there were never any boys.

They would sing and tell stories. And, after a while, we came to know them by their voices. The sisters all dressed in calico sundresses, but with sensible India-rubber Wellingtons, and the flopsy straw hats that old ladies wear. They would ply their bare fingers through the soil, plant, prune, and water.

Toward the end of the summer, they were in the garden less and the kitchen more. At two or three in the morning, as we crawled back through our windows, we could see into theirs. Catherine and Lucy worked at the table, Agatha stirred a bevy of bubbling pots.

We were sleeping in on a Saturday, just as we did every summer day, when we heard stomping on the porch and a clatter of glass. We dreamed similar dreams of milkmen, like in old TV shows, and a mother with an apron and a father with a pipe. But when we opened the door, there were eight bright canning jars. The sisters were already up the block, in their brown Wellies and long skirts, taking turns pulling a red wagon of jars.

We sat on the steps and smoked, watching them go door-to-door to friendlier neighbors, smiling and delivering preserves. We unscrewed the lids to use for ashtrays. There was no intention of eating their gift. And then, the porch was infused with aromas so wonderful and enchanting, so clean, we wondered how we'd ever filled ourselves with anything else.

We stamped out our butts and marauded the jars. No time for spoons.

We stuck in our fingers and licked them well. First pluot jelly, translucent as stained glass, turning from scarlet to gold when held to the light. The impossible tang of two fruits in one. Next, dark blueberry jam and the luscious tension of the berries between our teeth. And, hidden in the jar, surprising chunks of peach. This led very nicely to a corn relish in a confetti of colors from the torpedo onion, cilantro, and peppers both sweet and hot. And then, mushroom paté, though we didn't know then what it was. It was thick, exotic, and earthy. You could taste the soil in which they grew.

There were four other jars: red pickles, chutney, marmalade, and jam. We ate them all. We were sticky with sweet and dirty, and we wanted more. We had to know if it was the fruit itself or their talents that made it so delicious. We tried to climb the fence before the sisters headed homeward.

Our bare feet struggled against the slats and, together, we pulled the branches of their tree closer so the fruit hung on our side. Oh, it was beautiful! The globes were large and ripe, flushed and soft as baby cheeks. But, when we tried to pluck them, three peaches fell. They tumbled into their vegetable bed, rolling among the rapini and trembling pea shoots.

Before we had a chance to lament our fruit lost among the young turnips, there was a terrible crash.

As the sisters turned their wagon towards home, the remaining preserves in their wagon exploded. We hung on to the fence and watched the jars burst open sparking glass and spitting fruit. Our neighborhood was filled with salt and sugar and vinegar. Sticky bits of pickle and plum and a rainbow of other fruits spattered the sidewalk. The explosion echoed down the drive as our neighbors' gifts ruptured, the lids and rings ting-ting-tinging down the street.

The jars in their kitchen went off next. The volume and force blew the preserves through the windows. The garden beds were coated in macerated versions of themselves. The sisters were spangled with color. Jar shards shimmered in their hair. Agatha dumped chutney out of one boot. Catherine tied up her hair and shook the glass from her skirt. Lucy sat right down in the middle of the debris. She closed her eyes and prayed. We saw her lips moving; we couldn't hear the words.

Lucy rose and walked to the gate. She put her lips to the knothole and said, "We would have given you more, if only you had asked."

She picked up the three peaches and handed one to each of her sisters. They walked away together, leaving a red wagon of jagged glass and spoilt fruit. And, though we were still hungry, we didn't like them any more than when they'd first came.

Intercession

Rumors of a physical fight with the devil lead some young Catholic students to greater piety and others to malevolence.

My first year at Sacred Heart was the first year for many. So the events of that strange time we accepted more easily than the grown-ups, both from the resilience of youth and the fact we had no other time at the school to compare.

While other parish schools were struggling to stay open, ours had seen unrivaled increase in enrollment. Father Michael had come to Sacred Heart just the year before and through his intercession a bevy of young Dominican Sisters had agreed to come as well. They migrated to their newly-built small convent as joyfully as geese in full habit. Families from beyond our deanery, some with more than six children in grades K through 8, had enrolled their whole brood with hopes of the Sisters' influence instilling greater reverence.

Even in families of ten, most children had a dark and unpilled sweater vest for every day of the week. My one had faded to cadet blue, thin from laundering over and again.

I never had a problem being reverent. It's mostly just being quiet. Other boys in my class, the ones with good homes and confident catechism, still wiggled in the pews during Friday mass. But we all sat still for Father's homilies, tales of bloody accidents and miraculous interventions which saved the faithful from early deaths.

That Friday, the Deacon gave the homily instead of Father Michael. It was not until Father was preparing the Eucharistic altar that we could see the hard cast under the folds of his robe, the tape which secured his nose, or the plummy bruises blooming around his eyes. With stories of Padre Pio fresh in our young minds, it became clear to us what had befallen our priest. Father Michael was so holy that Satan had been unable to coax him with any temptation. In frustration, Satan had to resort to sending demons to simply beat him.

I imagined Satan had used the same tactics with my mother, who could not be provoked to despair or lose faith over anything my own father had done. She went to mass every day with a chapel veil for modesty. She wore her bruises without complaint, seeking holiness over pleasure or desire.

I heard Sister Agnes ask Father about his injuries, and all he said was, "The Devil does not want to lose this battle. He takes on many forms. I am patient, however, and I know Jesus, Our Lady, my Guardian Angel, and St. Francis are always with me."

In the lunchroom, we debated the demon fight. There was no question that it occurred, just the appropriate response. Mary A. and Mary O. (there were five Marys and two Marias in the third grade) assured us of Father Michael's eventual sainthood. In general, the girls felt we were called to greater holiness and the boys... well, the boys felt it best not to be so holy that the Devil would seek you out for particular attention.

On the way to Adoration, Sister Brigid had stopped by the statue of Saint Francis upon noticing what seemed to be a live mouse sleeping in his plaster palm. It was, unfortunately, in repose of the soul, having been skewered through the tail by a test pencil. The noise Sister made was most unmusical, but satisfied the perpetrator that the Devil would have no interest in beating him.

As the displays of irreverence increased, so did the consecrations to good. Those who did not seek a way to avoid demons' wrath sought to prove they were worthy of sainthood. Half the class was soap-scrubbed, rosary perpetually in hand, and intent on finding physical manifestation of the divine. Many fasted on bread and water until their small bodies were too depleted to do anything but pray at recess. Mary A. cut off her hair with kitchen shears to show that she had placed no importance on things of the flesh. (I think she must have seen this in a movie.) They pointed at oak galls and rust stains which were shaped in the image of Our Lady. They eagerly told the sisters of their visions of saints. But none of them, as far as I know, received a visitation. Mary-Clémence even achieved brief local fame for stigmata, tearfully holding her palms up to show the pooling blood, until the wounds were identified as self-inflicted by the sharp corner of her crucifix.

I can only imagine the mix of pride and puzzlement of which Father and the Sisters regarded us.

Even then, I could see that those aiming for holiness were going about it in an awful way. And, those attempting to escape perfection were already far from it – no little mouse needed to suffer to show the Devil he was not threatened.

Myself, I didn't change much. I was quiet. I didn't wait for miracles. I prayed that my mother would find some peace and I prayed for my confused classmates.

At night, when the demon did come for me, it would shake my bed until I tumbled out. Sometimes the demon appeared as a snarling wild dog, sometimes as a man, and sometimes unseen, just the scent of burnt timber. I would curl up like a mouse in the palm of St. Francis while the strikes landed like lead pipes against my back.

I'm not frightened anymore. But, ever since third grade, I've walked with a limp.

Lonely Exile

A prodigious boy escapes to an uninhabited island.

The dinghy moored itself at the shoreline of the tiny bright island without sound or ceremony. The boy simply stepped out, shook his wet head like a puppy in suburban sprinklers, and sat in the white sand to remove his sodden loafers. The journey had begun in the still-dark morning, amongst ill-tempered waves, but it had become quite pleasant by the time the dingy approached the isle.

When he looked in either direction, the boy could see the beach curve a few hundred meters along. It was unlike the seemingly endless Coast he'd visited earlier that summer, and he surmised that the island was very small. He had read a great many books, which had contributed to his problems, and surveyed a number of maps within those books, but could not readily identify the isle. The ship had been headed toward Saint Lucia, so he imagined he must be somewhere between Guadeloupe and La Desirade. Between Mary and Desire he was, as many a solitary young man might find himself. He retrieved the pillowcase from his vessel and placed its contents in a neat row aligned with his shoes: one corkscrew with a small folding knife meant for cutting a bottle's foil, two glass bottles of spring water, a half-full canister of vitamin pills, a peanut tin containing three matchbooks embossed with *Stella Maris* (the ship's name), a large spool of twine taken from the galley, and a silver comb engraved with the initials S.T.A. There was also a navy-and-cream-stripe wool blanket, too large to fit in the pillowcase, which he dutifully unfolded and spread to dry with the other items. Also, two oars.

His bare feet were as pale as the sand itself, but the heat radiated up through his soles and rose and dispersed through him like a nip of brandy. It was a sensation he'd encountered in his youth as part of a dietary reliance on discarded pearl onions, maraschino cherries, and pitted olives. At age six, however, he'd read that the most efficient daily diet consisted of eight open-faced peanut butter sandwiches, four glasses of whole milk, and a vitamin pill. And, the busy cook had happily supplied his request for this menu for the past five years. This solution may have come a year too late as, before age five, his temples turned silver-gray. This could have been attributed to undue stress or genetics, but most likely resulted from mineral deficiency associated with eating cocktail picks. Though the premature gray was an uncanny coincidence to the boy's given name, Sterling, it was his new distinguished appearance which gave way to the nickname "Senator." It was an adorable moniker for an earnest tot. Now 11, still earnest, he was through with it.

Now, until and unless he encountered someone else, he could choose any name or none for himself and the archipelago. Beyond the beach, the sea was an impossible blue. Inland, the flora and fauna were a riot of color. His mind tried to reconcile the delicate botanical plates from his library with the abundant fluttering and fragrant species. Having drunk a half-bottle of spring water and taken his daily vitamin, he removed his Topsiders from the line of items, reshod, and proceeded to explore. He recognized a large number of birds, including herons, sugarbirds, colibris, yellow-bellied bananaquit, and a rare type of wren he believed was last documented in 1914. Butterflies, beetles, and tiny lizards emerged at the lightest touch of a waxy leaf or bold bloom. The deeper into the tropical brush he walked, the steeper the climb seemed to be. The boy considered that the island might be an active volcano – though exquisite, uninhabited for good reason. He followed the sounds of the *Coereba flaveola* (banaquit), which were taking joy in piercing citrus fruit with their slender, curved bills, and discovered another delight: a waterfall which tumbled and effervesced through the lush vegetation all the way to the smallest of sandy coves where it rejoined the sea. He cupped his hands and drank. Then, following the satisfied local birds, selected several of the remarkably-hued fruits and perched on a rock to eat.

Having left his foil-cutter on the sand, he passed on the spiky jackfruit and chataigne, on the thick-skinned barbadine and melon, choosing instead fruits he could score with his thumbnail. A fallen squat banana proved to be the consistency of his missing peanut butter. It was sufficient, he thought, if not exotic. The boy bit into what appeared to be an apple, though a bit more heart-shaped and ruddy pink, to find the flesh as sweet and smooth as custard – for he had on occasion eaten holiday meals with his parents when home. There grew fruits he'd known only as highball garnishes: coconut, mango, and lime; those from Christmas stockings: tangerines, plump apricots, and pomegranates; and more from the plates of the leather-bound volumes: star-shaped carambola hanging among fragrant blossoms, the reptile-like spiny pale-green sour sop, and the preferable artichoke-shaped sweet sop which was plump with pudding-sweet pulp and little black seeds. He recalled the inked cross-section of these, the archival paper and precise labels, and felt his first pang of longing for the library. There were several thousand leather-bound volumes still unread. Around age four he'd begun at the shelves in the east corner and even then had found no rhyme no reason to their cataloguing. He harbored a suspicion that the books had not only been purchased by pound or by linear meter, but also that they were shelved only by the color of their leather covers. This gave the boy the distinct advantage of learning about a wide range of subjects without ever exhausting one. For Keats in cordovan binding was in a different section than Keats in cobalt, and the *Native Plants of the Caribbean* held no close geography to any other volume regarding that part of the world. His father took his brandy and selected pages of the daily in the library, but with the exception of his mother's holiday obligation to Dickens – a gilded red cover on the second shelf near the window seat – he had read in comfortable solitude. At parties, he was expected to recite

"Ode to Melancholy" or "Lines on the Mermaid Tavern" or to provide some other small act of prodigy. Neither his parents had seemed to care that the French word for pomegranate was "grenade" due to the fruit's jeweled seeds resemblance to shrapnel. His silvered-hair and small stature transformed the recitation of facts just such as this into a party trick.

The boy clambered back to the beach where his possessions remained aligned and untouched. He placed the corkscrew in his trouser pocket and proceeded to unwind the spool of twine, tie a triple line between to date trees, and halve the wool blanket over the line to create a simple tent. A mongoose family scaled the date tree, curious and watchful. The boy named the large one Rico, the smaller two Archer and Victor, for it was his island and things could have names or not at his own discretion.

At dusk, he built a fire with the fallen fronds. At night, the sky and sea were each so clear it was impossible to see where one ended and the other began. The boy did not see this effect. After much rowing and exploring and exuberant consumption of fruit, he'd finally succumbed to sleep. He was awoken many hours later, arms sore but otherwise hale, by the scurry of a great magenta crab across one bare foot. The isle was full of wonders fatal and benign. While his bibliologic voracity provided him with an advantage on most things animal, mineral, and vegetable, there were certain attractions unique to the island, items which most certainly had not been catalogued. An ornamental tree, nine meters high, was rich with ruby fruit which burst open on its own accord when ripe to reveal three large seeds and creamy yellow pulp. He could not know that these were also rife with toxicity if eaten before full maturity. And, there were unfamiliar fishes in the cove, swimming so slowly and in such proximity to the surface as to be suicidal. These were sleek at first glance, but cached four rows of exquisite teeth. Briefly, the boy himself considered what he did not know, and decided there was no other way to study it than by the practical application.

The boy breakfasted on sea grapes and sorrel and a type of purple-red plum. He chewed thoughtfully on a length of sugar cane he'd found in a small thatch of the stuff on the northerly side. The sugar sustained his climb to the center of the island, where he choose the highest tree at its highest point and scaled it like a slender mongoose. At first, the ocean appeared brilliant and uninterrupted all around him. And then, on the edge of his field of vision, the archipelagic reality began to emerge. Other green islands were visible, other boats nearing their shores, white and geometric against the undulating blue.

This is my island, he insisted with the dramatic conviction of the young. *I'll live here forever.* And on this point he was true.

For although one of the white ships was indeed his *Stella Maris*, its occupants had already ceased searching for their missing passenger. In the clear waters of Marie-Galante had been found a capsized dinghy and the body of a young man with unmistakable temples of grey. His parents, having not understood Senator much in the decade or so they'd shared, could not possibly conceive of his eternal adventures enjoying the fruits of an island of his own.

My Better Nature

*In the depth of winter, a lycanthrope
struggles to reconcile his two selves.*

It was February and the melt was months away. There was a certain quiet, a lonely beauty of which my telling cannot do justice. Imagine the word tree or swing the only thing on the page. Surrounded by white, the few things left showing become objects of art. Snow ribbed the overturned vessels stacked at the silent boathouse. The lakes were deeply drifted; we had a falling feeling until our boots finally touched ice. Our tracks were deep. By the time we reached home, they were already covered with fresh snow.

The sun burned copper when she led me to the garage. I was too spent and sorry to argue. Perhaps for her safety, perhaps for mine. Perhaps she just wanted to let me die.

I knew the pain I'd caused. In flats along the parkway, families—normal families—were having birthday parties, cooking stew, playing bridge, and mending mittens. But they weren't packing their thermoses and skates for the warming house and hockey boards or heading to Matt's for a burger and a three-two beer. Normal families were staying home. The Catholics took to wearing medals of Saint Hubert. After the attacks increased, even the Lutherans adopted him.

I climbed into the trunk. She showed me a straw-like tube jimmied through a hole in the floor.

"You'll be able to breathe," she said. "It's just until dawn."

We didn't speak much anymore.

I curled fetal and she closed the lid. A little orange light crept through the cracks. I closed my eyes and tried to remember fairy tales Mormor told me as a child. Soon, the trunk went black. I couldn't remember the morals of the stories. I scratched and kicked. Though the metal was bitterly cold, I was sweating. My heart throbbed disyncopated and frantic. Blood pumped hot. The tube slipped from my slick hands out the hole. A creamy light shone through. The bristles under my tongue were first.

I was braver and hungrier. I could not be contained. And these modern cars are equipped with panic handles in the trunk. You don't even need opposable thumbs.

I was still my other self when she found me. She followed bloody paw prints which had eaten up the snow, punctuated by inedibles: bit of denim, silver medal, toddler's shoe. My lips were greasy with fat, my whiskers sticky with frosting. She cupped my muzzle and turned my face to hers. I growled her away, but there was no menace in it. My tongue was singed. Something was stuck in my canines.

She sighed. Like the mouse prying the lion's thorn, she plucked the blue birthday candle from my teeth.

"He had just turned three."

The hunters were coming. I smelled them. I stood on all fours, belly full and taut, and licked her ear as gently as I could. I ran from the warming house, bounding through the drifts. I headed for the woods, trying not to think of the man I would be at dawn. A man naked and alone.

New Alchemy

In the near future, the world is challenged and changed by a pandemic of a fierce propagation of raw metals in the blood.

It started with a gleam. Something golden under the skin. Beautiful, almost. A spangle of dots came next, like brass-colored freckles, which would oxidize green and blue and black. By then, the metals were so heavy in the blood, it was a hard to get a needle through. And, once the eyes and mouth were coated, it was too late to change.

Things were different before you were born.

With all the books and movies about vampires, zombies, werewolves, and such, not to mention all the environmental crises, people were ready for an apocalypse. At least, they were entertained by packing MREs and water jugs and buying weapons at Wal-Mart. Some people traded their cash for gold, some grew their own vegetables. The wealthy had their own blood saved a pint at a time and preserved by cryogenics.

Perhaps the idea of an apocalypse was better than the real thing. People aren't that open to change. Or, perhaps they had a desire to fight an outside enemy. Not their own blood.

We called it Plating. There was no cure and there was no vaccine. And transfusion was the only treatment. You'd go to the bank and have a couple of pints taken out and spun in the big centrifuge, so the base metals would sink to the bottom and the rest could be piped back in. But they couldn't ever salvage enough to fill you back up. And there wasn't enough clean blood to go around. Plating didn't stop people from having babies or car wrecks or cancer. The banks needed their regular blood supply and about ten times more to keep up.

The government programs didn't help much. To keep Plating at bay, you had to go to the bank about once a week. Not a day after you were clean, the metallic taste, like drinking from a can of off-brand soda, would be back. The private blood banks sprang up nearly overnight, so did health insurance. And so did black-market blood, homemade centrifuges, and sidewalk zealots.

Everybody had a theory: nuclear energy, petroleum in the food, exposure to plastics, wrath of God. Everywhere you looked, there was another promised remedy: magnets, pure living, prayer.

Plating became apparent in the elderly first. They had an opalescent shimmer, as if the glow of youth was returning, but then they became more spotted and even slower than before. Open a vein, and you'd find only ore. It was a process, almost like chroming a bumper. The body cleaned and etched itself inside out, and turned from nickel-color to copper to a dark silvered shine. With enough metal, people transformed into cast statues of themselves. At the park, there were parked wheelchairs holding iron ladies. There were homeless growing lead beards as they slept.

Since children weren't yet showing signs, some assumed it was a sexual or moral affliction – that our indiscretions were written in our blood – a mercurial letter A. But then almost everyone got the Plating, and the only thing you knew for sure was who had enough money to afford treatment. And even those few who had stored their own blood away for just such an event learned that the cryostat was locked for at least ten years. Or, it was a sham and their blood had been sold or tossed. No one expected the apocalypse so soon.

There was power and water. The grocery stores were stocked, the subways ran. Things became unhinged in other ways. Permanent ports were placed in the crooks of peoples' elbows to make the draw faster. Banks, both blood and money, were massed to near-riot. The back-alley blood work grew common and it was not unusual to see duct tape where a sterile bandage should have been. People were a quart low. They floated palely through daily routines, sleeping more and rushing less. Missing trains and social cues, looking in the mirror for sequin-like spots on the skin. As blue-tinged ghosts, they tried to extend the time between each blood buy and spin.

We were just paycheck-to-paycheck before the Plating began. We didn't have much, and what we had couldn't cover the weekly banks. I was holding on fine – about eight months along before I even had a glimmer on my skin. The doctors think it was the increased blood volume that diffused the metal; I think it had something to do with you. Your father, of course, was more advanced. His temples were wiry, prematurely gray, his skin cast in shadows. I know he'll be so happy when he finally sees you.

Labor was hard and the hospital hectic. You were born perfect, pink-tinted and healthy weight. When I brought you home, before I could even lay you in the dresser drawer we'd made into a tiny bed, I saw you Plating. You opened your gold-flecked eyes and regarded me with such trust and calm. I knew I couldn't take you to the crowded panic of the bank. I couldn't subject your chubby arm to needle draw after draw. And, I didn't need to.

You were plated in waves of flickering light. Your little body became heavy and more bright. You were covered in gold flake, as delicate and lovely as butterfly scales. And, when I polished you smooth, you didn't cry at all.

As it turns out, you and the others don't have blood, or need blood, at all.

And someday, I'm sure, your father will cast off his statue, and emerge as golden and perfect as you.

The Still-Sleeping World

In 1938, a border crossing in the Alps determines the fate of Jewish passengers. Can, and will, God intervene?

There was no sound but the panting of the engine as our train wound its way through the snow-laden mountainside. In the dark early morning, the snow glistened blue in its passing light.

I held Josepha so that my mother could stitch Shoshanah's skirt. I remember sitting on the floor of the compartment with my sisters. Josepha was not yet one, Shoshanah was seven, and I was ten. My mother turned the jeweled rooster over and over in her hand before sewing it into Shoshanah's hem.

"Why the *sechvi*, mama?" I'd asked. "You have so many pretty brooches."

My mother took the pins from her mouth. "This animal has a special place in our family and in our faith... The Talmud says, 'When you hear the rooster crowing at dawn, you should say *Blessed is the One who has given understanding to the rooster.'* Our Torah encourages us to cherish wisdom. And, God has blessed the rooster with the unique ability to perceive the dawn of a new day, and to crow it loudly to the still-sleeping world."

My father entered our compartment from the hall, hat in hand, but my mother continued. "Remember *sechvi* does not only mean rooster... it also refers to the human heart. Just as the rooster distinguishes between the light of day and the darkness of the night, so too the human heart should distinguish between those ideas which bring light into the world, and those which bring darkness."

My father kissed her on the forehead. "We're at the border... Don't be afraid, darling, it will just be a formality. They'll check our visas and let us on our way."

"Mama's not afraid of anything," I said.

The steam squealed from the train as it slows to a stop. The porter knocked on our cabin door and asked us to detrain. He asked us to bring our papers and our bags. He had asked it kindly, but my father still asked him if there was a problem, as if it had been an unreasonable or unexpected demand.

"No sir, the porter said. "It often happens this way. Everything will be fine."

Our family stepped off the train together. Shoshanah and I held hands. Our tracks were deep in the snow as we approached the border crossing. A guard demanded our papers and Papa handed a sheaf of passports and visas to him.

Without even looking at the papers in his hand, the guard ordered two other officers to escort my father away. They led him to a small concrete building. My mother clutched Josepha to her chest and ran after them, but she was held back.

"Joseph! Joseph! Joseph!" she yelled, kicking and flailing. Josepha, his namesake, was wailing, too.

Three guards took us to a separate bunker. "We need to check you thoroughly... take off everything," they demanded my mother. And then, through my mother's protests, they demanded the same of Shoshanah and me.

We were just little girls. I will not say what happened next in the ugly yellow light of that bunker. Somehow, by the time the snow began to fall again, we were returning to the train.

Shoshanah and I met in the dining car. Her cheeks were flushed bright pink and her eyes were glittering. From the window, we could see my mother and baby sister trekking through the snow back to the train. They left no footprints. My mother was also flushed and bright-eyed. My cheeks felt hot when I finally could embrace her.

"Oh, my darlings, I'm so sorry," she whispered. "But we must be grateful they let us go! We are all together, thank God. And we'll be in a safe place soon... "

We sat at a small table and the same elderly porter came by with a tea tray. Steam rose as he poured three cups.

"Where's papa?" my sister asked him.

My mother looked concerned, but just reassured her that he was on his way back.

Shoshanah nodded toward the porter and said, "*He* knows."

He then poured himself a cup of tea and joined our table. He patted my mother's hand in a comforting way and, as he did, their two hands together emitted an eerie glow. He cupped her hands together and poured hot tea, then milk, right into her palms. The liquid vanished without even touching her lips.

"This isn't right, isn't possible... " she said. And then, after only a moment of consideration, "We're gone, aren't we? We never came back from that bunker."

"Of course we came back, mama," I countered "We're right here!"

"Dead and gone are not the same," the porter said.

"We're not dead," Shoshanah stated matter-of-factly, in the way only a seven-year-old can.

"You have very intuitive girls." The porter leaned in and spoke to us in a low voice, sharing a secret. "The way I understand it, young ladies, is that God never intended for our bodies and souls to be separate. And, we all look forward to the eventual divine reunion. But, sometimes, God perceives that the future of certain bodies may be too much for those souls to bear. It's by his grace that, for a little time on earth, the body goes one direction and the soul another."

"What's going to happen to us?" I asked him.

"Well, miss, your forms are on another train... headed for someplace God would like to spare you. So, me surmising what happens in those camps goes against His plan to keep your soul safe."

He stirred his tea. "A soul such as myself can still feel and taste and touch the world, only in a different way... The catch, of course, is that I'm not sure where or what my old body is doing. So, it will come as great surprise to me when I pass on, wherever I am, and this soul and that body are reunited."

My mother stroked Josepha's cheek and the baby's skin shone luminously where touched. Shoshanah patted her braids, sweater, and skirt to see what of her was still there. She reached for her pleated hem. There was a slit in the place the brooch had been hidden. Her fingers could go right through.

"But where's our papa?" we insisted.

A gunshot echoed from the small building by the border crossing. We are all quiet and still.

"He's not like us," the porter replied. "He won't wait."

Our train continued through the Alps as sunlight began to break. In the distance, a rooster crowed. The mountainside was a blaze of color as the sunrise reflected against fresh snow.

The Voracious Reader

The best editor may just well be a bookbug.

The best stories, I have been told, are located exactly on the second shelf of the Mystery and Suspense section (authors C through H) in the Red Bud Public Library at 112 Bloom Street. The books of Cain, James M. through Highsmith, Patricia have been lovingly edited to the last apostrophe. And while the 11,450 other titles are under excellent care, they are not under the same exacting dissemination.

Thysanura are found under the fabric, bark, and boards of much of Randolph County. And the library book bindings, curtains, wallpaper are no exception. What is an exception is Roger the *Lespisma sacchrina*. (That's "silverfish" for those of you not familiar with Dewey Decimal Classification 595.7.) Roger hatched under the cover of Agatha Christie's first novel, and has been quite the reader ever since.

Roger's brothers and sisters are secretive and are usually most active at night, hiding in cracks and crevices, content to chew on glue and endpapers. His taste is more discerning. Having grown up in the suspense classics of the 1930's, he has firm opinions on the art of fiction. Luckily for the Red Bud patrons, the most terrible things to consume are the most delicious.

Like the sweet comfort of Twinkies and cherry cola, so are the fatty and syrupy passages devoured by Roger. His belly has rounded with the consumption of so many unnecessary "ly"-ending adjectives. Honestly, some writers can't let a sentence go by without one! And, the wardrobe descriptions! In Roger's opinion, detailing a fedora down to the last feather in the band doesn't constitute character development. Considering the contemporary works shelved alongside the classics, Roger has a pretty good idea how times have changed. He's sensitive to the misogyny and racial bias in the hard-boiled stories, and tends to chew up the epithets therein. More often than not he spits them back out.

Some meals are for literary merit, some for personal preference. Roger has kindly removed the drier of the Sherlock stories. He's taken a fine tooth to the talented Ripley, in order to make Tom's sexual preference less ambiguous. Contrariwise, he's nipped a bit at Chandler when morals got too fast and loose. Not too much, you understand, just enough to keep it on Illinois public shelves.

Upon discovering that *And Then There Were None* and *Ten Little Indians* were actually the same book, Roger ate the entirety of the latter. Fortunately, he was not exposed to the other alternate, and highly offensive, title. That hefty meal made him sluggish for weeks after. It took considerable effort to lift his listless antennae and slip them under the desired page.

He did not, however, find much to munch in *The Maltese Falcon*. Roger envied Hammett a bit. He simply snacked on the page numbers and read with appreciation.

Roger was only a couple of pages into Rebecca when he was disturbed. Mary West, accredited librarian and the little library's sole employee, was in early. The fluorescents flickered, but Roger was no longer as fast as his sleek scurrying siblings. Mary's heels clicked through Fiction, and the list of inter-county transfers fluttered in her pale hand. As she searched the D's for du Maurier, Roger attempted to sneak past. He was not quick enough. Would this be his big sleep?

Mary giggled girlishly as Roger's three long tail-like projections tickled her palm. "Oh, you nuisance!" she said with a smile.

She gently deposited Roger outside in a patch booming over with blue violets and goldenrods. He blinked in the sunlight and his silvery body for once was still. The riot of floral colors and scents was curious and intoxicating. In his heart, he bid the second shelf a long goodbye.

Roger's abrupt retirement from his editorship was bittersweet. His legs twitched, unsure of what next to pursue. He grew warm in his recognition that he'd made an improvement in the reading life of generations to come in Red Bud. Roger shimmied under a layer of bark, unaware of thousands and thousands of libraries and bookstores past Randolph County.

Millions and millions of mysteries circulating unedited all over the world.

Written on the Skin

An exceptional tattooed lady draws a true admirer.

.

We had a lot in common, Lola and me. We joined the 10-in-1 the same year, when we were both still kids, but the management seemed to neither notice nor mind. We each got paid $150 a week, better than almost anybody else in the company. At least four times what she'd make working in a clerical pool, Lola had said. We both liked rock candy. And, like the pressure cooker I'd seen at the World's Fair, we both had a steam release. Lola had laughed when I'd told her, but it was true: just the way that salesman's thumb pressed the regulator weight on a nozzle next to the lid handle, we'd each found a way to let out some of what made us different so that we wouldn't blow up. Neither of us slept much.

The Parkes-Maximus American Circus and Museum of Wonders wasn't such a bad place. I got three squares and a bed from March to November and I made enough money to hold me over on the off-season. There were rules for Parkes-Maximus employees, mostly about fraternization between the equestriennes and ballet girls with the likes of us. But the born curiosities kept to themselves, like the wolf-man and the half-lady. The management treated them pretty well cause they'd be hard to replace. The made curiosities kept with the made. The novelty acts kept to themselves. And, the gaffed acts, why those were just cons. They might fool the audience, but none of the rest of us would play a hand of cards with 'em. There were folks in the circus who were jerks and folks who were decent enough, just like any job anywhere. And then there was

Lola. She was so kind; it was hard to reconcile her sweet face with the illustrated rest of her.

Lola wore a floor-length silk robe in spring and a velvet robe in fall. Underneath she wore a green satin bathing costume that ended about four inches above her knees. Among all ten attractions in the tent, Lola was the one that seemed to most amaze. More than the blind young snake-charmer, more than the bearded lady, more than the two pygmies from a far pagan land. Even more than what I could show 'em. Once she untied her robe, the tent fell silent. If across her shoulders was tattooed the Last Supper, folks would see the eyes of Christ regarding them with tender mercy. If down one arm was a soldier erecting our nation's flag, why any man who'd ever served would see himself and his fallen friends. Housewives saw themselves and their own in the Madonna and child. Little boys saw themselves in Tom Mix on her thigh. Lola's body showed people the truth about themselves. Every inked inch of her a wonder.

On my platform, I'd hold a bare bulb in my hands and folks'd watch it incandesce at my touch. I'd roll up my sleeves to show there was no wire or trick to it. The bulb would grow brighter the more I pressed, casting the rest of the tent in shadows and nobody but Lola and me in the light.

I'd kissed her once. It was the day she'd turned nineteen. Her silk robe had slipped off one decorated shoulder and I couldn't help myself. When I kissed a collection of dark stars, the black outline of a crescent moon appeared on her shoulder.

Nobody got to wise to Lola's abilities. We weren't in any one city longer than a week, and Lola traveled with a proper tattooing machine, sort of an adaptation of Edison's electric pen. There was a reservoir for ink, and a tubular handle with a little gauge and a reciprocal needle. On Sunday nights, when the show was dark, we could hear the hum of the electromotor as Lola passed it across her skin, transforming old portraits into new. What I knew was that there was no ink in it at all. All Lola needed was to be touched and her illustrations would tell the story. It was impossible for her to lie.

Back on my cot, electrons danced between my fingertips. As I thought about Lola, the camp lights would ebb and glow. I could even make her whirring needle stop if I put my mind to it.

One Sunday, I went to see if she needed help. I could be the one at least to pass the empty needle across the apostles on her back. Lola handed me the armature. She was quiet, just swinging one dear decorated foot to the needle-whirr and eating rock candy. Quiet was fine. I knew her and she knew me. After a while, other faces appeared and other flowers grew and other flags waved on Lola. And, when I looked down at her lovely leg, I saw a face I knew. The blind Indian was drawn above her ankle just as clear and true as a photograph. As she flexed her little foot, he raised his reed and the illustrated basket opened. Instead of a cobra uncurling to the imaginary music, a flurry of hearts and stars emerged. They drifted up the curve of her calf and under her robe where I could not see. Then Lola's own silhouette, which I'd recognize in any form, arose from the basket, each fine finger curled and coaxing the drawn Indian. The real Lola was blushing. That much I could still see, her rosy hue cast across every story she wore.

The sparks flew from my fingertips radiant green. My hair stood on end and even my woolen socks pulled away from my feet. The nearest town was almost mile out from the field where our tents were staked. And still, all those regular people in their regular homes had their lights go out that night. All those folks, awake in the deepest dark and quiet, not sure what was going to happen next.

Fables Domestic

The Changing Room

*Things go awry when an ambitious young woman
infiltrates an exclusive country club.*

C.W. usually takes number 6. She leaves two cocktail rings, the valet tag and lip gloss in a leather wristlet, but puts her BlackBerry in the pocket of her robe. Hanna leaves a Birkin filled with goodies—a Symthson diary, black AmEx, 'scrips— in number 11 on Mondays and Thursdays. And an unnamed patron with an impeccable silver bob favors number 18. The shoes she leaves are insanely good, if I was lucky enough to be her size.

I take 24 in the corner. But I won't tell you what I keep in it yet.

You really don't need to bring anything here. In the atrium, there is always hot tea and yerba maté, fresh fruit and a crisp stack of magazines. The girls provide a warm robe and slippers and a little brass key that matches a numbered brass plate on your locker. Just drop your car with the valet and give your signature for all else. You don't need anything, but it's amazing the things people bring.

The moneyed are trusting, I told Brewster. Just last month, I returned a handbag from Filene's Basement to Ralph Lauren. And the tony catering spot next door took my personal check without asking for an ID or running it through a machine. It's as if you wouldn't even know they existed unless you were one of them, so of course you can afford it.

When I joined Highsmith, there was a whole docket of paperwork to fill out. But when I gave the guest services manager my check, she simply folded it into her appointment book.

"Do what you need to do and get out of there," said Brewster. "Get the hell out before they try to cash that check."

It takes time, I told him. I need to learn routines. Hanna, for example, takes off her jewelry before a massage so it doesn't get slick with lavender oil. C.W. doesn't wear her rings to her appointments with the new young pro.

It's not too hard to fit in. Old money, that's what you want to be. Old money has a certain look. Don't bother with the runway stills in *Bazaar*, take note of what the philanthropists are wearing. I chose a camelhair coat, oversize sunglasses, a pair of ballerina flats, and a burnt-orange "Kelly" bag. The faux-Hermès stays tucked snug under my arm, so you can't see the crooked stitching. My studs are CZ.

I go straight to the ladies' lounge without opening my coat. There's no point in wearing anything underneath. If I wanted to dress like them, though, I'd wear one color from head to toe. Preferably ivory or cream. You have to be well-off to look immaculate in a color that's so easily stained. Old money shies from color at the argument of quality. If you get regular manicures, you shouldn't need polish. Fingernails and toenails should be the healthy pink of a seashell. Polish is tacky, acrylic tips are tacky, logoed handbags and piss-colored diamonds are tacky.

A woman should have the resources and leisure to take care of herself. As far as they know, I do.

My hair is blown-out daily. I choose smoothies of anti-oxidant rich berries. I allow myself to be lulled by the water-play in the fountain, by the hush-hush of slippers in the corridor. In between treatments, there's a steam room and an endless pool. As I relax in the atrium, flipping through *Philanthropy Magazine*, the ladies are escorted down one hall to the med-spa, down another for wet treatments, another for the salon.

New money women gossip incessantly about their husbands, their help, and each other. They look for their own photos in the social pictures of the metro magazines. But even I know that a lady should only be in the paper twice—upon her marriage and upon her death. My silence is taken as old money manners, which is just as well. When I do speak, I am amicable to everyone. I am gracious to the manicurists, the juice girl, the laundry girl. I remember everyone's name and thank them sincerely. It would be tacky not to.

When you are given such thoughtful attention, you want to be lovely enough to deserve it. Everything and everyone is nice. The lockers don't even need vents. In most changing rooms, they need to make sure your unaired gym clothes don't go skunky. Here, you leave your spent tennis whites or yoga pants in a little mesh bag, and a girl brings them back cleaned and pressed on a hanger.

The changing room here smells like Boucheron, brass polish and vanilla bean. Brewster smells of charred coffee and curdled milk. His polo gets soaked when he empties the garbage at Sweet Bean, and I swear that stink won't wash out. Brewster makes $7.75 an hour and splits the tip jar. He just doesn't understand.

I don't want to squander all of the amenities that Highsmith Resort Club & Spa has to offer. Though I haven't told Brewster, I slipped my check right out of that drawer when no one was looking. It will take them a little longer to realize it's gone, and apologetically ask for another, than it would to bounce the first. I haven't yet tried the restaurant's signature salmon and micro-greens or any of the seven types of yoga at the Health & Wellness Pavilion. I haven't stayed in the villas. I did, however, sign for a couple of great pieces from the boutique, so I'll have something to wear besides the robe.

Today, as I make my way across the lawn, I see Brewster. He's pacing outside the gates and waiting for me to come out.

His arms, ropy from hoisting bags of beans, strain his knit shirt. Brewster's ready for his cut and ready for me to come home. But I don't think that security will buzz in an angry guy in a dirty barista apron. Even if he has a bit of a temper, Brewster's not stupid. He won't interfere if there's still a chance of getting the goods.

"Get them when they're down to their drawers," he said. "If a women is as classy as all that, you could slip a ring right off her hand during a mud bath, or whatever it is, and she's not gonna run half-naked after you."

Honestly, Brewster just doesn't get it.

Still, I skip Pilates in the pavilion and head back to the changing room before Brewster can see me. And there, kneeling in front of number 24, is the laundry girl. She's got the lock to my Kelly bag in her right hand.

Now, the lock should be engraved with the word "Hermès" and a number, and this number should match one engraved on each of two keys. Lottie knows this and I know this. Just the same way the little brass key clipped to my sleeve is engraved with "24." Lottie—that's the laundry girl—I've always remembered to thank her by name. The counterfeit handbag is a moot point, though, as Lottie has two pages from *Philanthropy* clutched in her other hand. On one I'd kept a careful ledger of the comings and goings of the other guests: when and what they would leave in their lockers. On the other (and this list was almost as long) I chronicled Brewster's exploits, as leverage in case he decided to rat on me.

The old me wouldn't know quite how to handle this, but the new me feels absolutely clear. I focus on the *H* embroidered on Lottie's knit shirt and I take pity on her. It reminds me of Brewster's sad work shirt and its little stitched heart and coffee bean. I take a deep yogic breath before I speak.

"Lottie, do you need some help?"

She startles and drops the bag.

"Lottie," I say with infinite patience, "if you needed bus fare to get home, you only need to have asked."

"Oh no, miss," she says. "I just came to hang your cleaning in your locker."

"Thank you…"

"And all of this just fell out."

"I see."

Lottie smoothes the lists flat, then hands me the orange Kelly, my un-cashed check, a hair clip, an earring.

Poor girl, I think. *Once you're caught going through a member's personal belongings, it would be hard to get another job at a nice place like Highsmith. It would be hard to get minimum wage at Sweet Bean.*

So I won't say anything about it. I'm a private person, really, and I don't want to bring undue attention upon myself.

"Thank you, Lottie."

I put the papers in the bag, the bag on the hook, the clip in my hair and the earring in my pocket.

"You're welcome, miss." Then her face flushes pink and sweaty as if she'd steeped in the steam room. And she goes.

It's getting late. The ladies come and empty their lockers. They have pressing social engagements. I sit in a dim corner of the changing room, turning the earring over in my hand. See, if there's a rash of theft, no one will keep their valuables in their lockers anymore. They might just leave the club altogether. And girls like Lottie could lose their jobs. And, eventually, they'll be looking for me. But one earring out of a pair, that's not a theft, that's just carelessness. It's bound to turn up.

Once it's dark, I'll pry the diamonds out of Hanna's Fred Leighton piece. And I'll be able to properly pay my membership dues.

The door to the changing room opens. I expect it's the laundry girl's return, but it's the prematurely-silver socialite. I see her though she doesn't see me. She takes an oversized hobo bag from number 18 and drops in something shiny. Then, after giving the room a quick scope, she grabs a stack of freshly laundered towels and two pairs of slippers and shoves them in, too. It's a shame. I'd think that a woman with shoes like hers would have better taste.

The door of number 18, like the rest of the changing room, is immaculate. Slick and polished, no breathing holes. The little brass plate catches the light. And, before she can see me, I've decided to take care of this myself. Taking towels is just plain tacky. We can't have that kind of thing here. It's an atmosphere of trust.

The Cleaver

A girl survives the Holocaust by virtue of a butcher's kindness.

Underneath the smell of fat, blood, and salt, Isa can smell the sun. It radiates from Bruno who, in defiance of his name, is as golden as the Aryan ideal. And, despite his kindnesses, she's jealous of his freedom to enjoy the weather.

It's July now. The storage garret is sweltering. Westfalian landschinken and links of landjägers crowd the curing hooks. The hams and sausages mostly repel her, though there is some comfort in their camouflage.

Still, Isa's luckier than most.

There are entire families hidden in spaces smaller than this. Families with little food or water, with crying infants and terrible decisions to make.

She's survived so far due to her dry, delicate wit, what her father called attic salt. And, of course, attic faith. " Now faith is the substance of things hoped for," he told her, "the evidence of things not seen. "

She doesn't speak to Bruno often, but she sees daily evidence of his affection. There are food packages, modest but fine, delivered before sunrise and after sunset. Books in German, Hebrew, English, and Czech. Candles. A pitcher of water in the middle of the night.

Isa's pragmatic. She's certainly has time to think about things. Though her feelings for Bruno could be afforded to dependence, or loneliness, or gratitude, that's not all this is. Given another time and place she would feel the same admiration. She wonders at Bruno's strength, both his physicality and his character. His arms rope-muscled from his daily work, and a butcher's work itself, belie a gentleness. It's as if she's a wounded-wing bird he's cradled from the windowsill. But it's more than that, too. She feels it when their eyes meet over lighting a match, the way their fingers brush when the candle passes hands.

She's come to know this stranger by his gestures: a kosher meal wrapped in butchers' paper, a rose-scented cake of soap, news he gleans from the gossiping patrons. Bruno takes great risk to bring her these pleasures—to her they are not so very small.

It's been weeks since Papa left to go looking for her sister Lisabet, and no word from him. No news overheard. It's just Isa and the charcuterie sharing the dark, salty space.

This isn't kosher, she thought the first day, and laughed out loud at the turn of phrase. Papa, Lisabet, and the stranger all shot her awful looks at the inappropriate mirth. It wasn't right to laugh when so much was at stake. It can't be right to feel the flush of love when there's been so much loss. But then, nothing's been right since that first yellow Jude star was stitched to her sweater.

Under other circumstances, Isa may not be tempted, as she is now, to take a piece from the tref ham and revel in the new taste. Desperate times are the true tests of our faith. Is it better to starve than partake of the forbidden? An endless series of days unfold in the near dark, with the seeming inevitability of iron-heeled jackboots kicking in the attic door. And darkness grows in Isa with each day she comes to know Bruno and what cannot be.

She's come to live by this stranger's routine. She anticipates the whir of the knife wheel. She waits for the lock of the shop doors the way a patient waits for the tap of the fingernail on a vial of morphine.

Isa can hear him closing up shop below. She cups a candle and strikes a match before she can lose the ambient light. Bruno whispers her name.

He enters the attic, sits on the floor, and sets down a bundle of white cotton carefully.

"Isa." Her name rests on his lips like a prayer. "Officers were in the shop today. Could you hear?" He doesn't wait for a response. "I will do everything in my ability to protect you,

Isa…. But if you hear boots which aren't mine upon these steps…"

He cannot bear to say more. Instead, he leans over the flame and kisses Isa. For one brief sparking moment, she can feel everything. It's a kiss full and wet with regret and longing and finality.

Bruno opens the folded apron to reveal a small bottle of bleach and a butcher's knife. "Whatever happens, don't let them take you, Isa."

She presses her face to Bruno's cheek, his tears hot on her lashes. For the first time since hiding, Isa allows herself to cry, too. Her love is pure. It's not susceptible to violence, not capable of being profaned.

When Bruno leaves the attic, she turns the well-honed knife over in her hand. A terrible decision to make. To cleave means to cling faithfully, Isa thinks. To cleave means to split apart.

She pulls her hair up tight with a ribbon and hacks with the knife until all of the long locks are strewn at her feet. She takes off her shirtdress. Using the apron to cover her eyes, she pours bleach over her hair. Wet-headed, Isa uses a bent pin to rip the stitches out of those sickly yellow stars. Isa waits. She scrubs with a soap cake. She rinses over and again from the pitcher to the bowl.

By morning, she's as blond as Garbo and smells like a rose. Isa smoothes out her dress and ties on the apron. She pushes the door open, reveling in the draft. Even the scent of fresh blood from the shop below is a blessing after months of salt and smoke. She ventures farther onto the steps and breathes deeply. Bruno turns, startled to see her out of context and out of color. He smiles.

"I'm sorry to keep you waiting. The shop has been so busy lately," Bruno tells his morning customers. "It may be fortunate that my widowed cousin will be coming to town soon. Perhaps she'll be able to help."

Delicates

A tenuous relationship begins at a late-night laundromat.

There was nothing natural about it. The chrome and enamel and melamine were too bright for the hour and too clean for the neighborhood. All-Nite Kennedy Launderette pink neon tubing looped in enthusiastic cursive. A black kid with jawbreaker-size plastic hair baubles peered in the washer windows as if ogling pies in an automat, and her braids clattered against the glass. Laun-der-ette, it makes a better name for a girl than a coin-op.

The girl relished her one-night pass to stay up so late, unlike the adult patrons who merely had a temporary respite from someplace worse. The homeless from JFK Park. The blonde who, last month, tried to manage folding shirts with one arm in a hard cast. And me, who can't sleep. And, after giving most everything I had away after Nora left, well, I've got to run a load every night anyway.

The blonde has a soft sling now. I can tell she's still in pain. She gingerly removes her boots and places them on top of the machine. She smiles as her bare toes meet the cold linoleum.

It's the first time I've seen her smile. Her mouth is as plump and tender as a bruised plum. There's a black seam of dried blood on her bottom lip.

"This isn't your usual night," I say. And right away I realize how wrong it is, how stalker-like I sound.

"Ah have a lawt of lawndery," she drawls softly. Laundry is three syllables.

I'm making her uncomfortable. She drums her fingers on the washer lid. The clink of her ring startles us both. She looks down at it as if she doesn't quite know how it got there in the first place. And, wordlessly, she slips it off and drops into a bottle of bluing.

Washers rumble overstuffed, sneakers thump in dryers, quarters jangle in the change machine tray. I want to stay in this place. In this quiet eye. The air around her is honeysuckle, salt, and soil, and if I step away I'm lost in the sizing, bleach, and canned fragrance of soap flakes. I try to think of something to say. I want to justify my nearness.

Her hair is pale and her skin is pale and freckles are spangled across her nose and shoulders and everywhere. Wonderful. Her ears are pink and perfect as a conch shell. Her dress is old-fashioned, a thin calico that clings to her in places as though it were damp. It's spattered a bit with mud or something at the edges.

My buzzer goes. I'm rescued to a purpose. I can empty the dryer slowly, fold slowly. When I drop the warm bundle on the folding table, she's eating laundry powder.

She cups it from the box the way a child would scoop snow, and eats it with the same novelty and pleasure.

"Pica," she says.

"Pete," I correct, and stick out my hand. She laughs and shakes it. I can feel the detergent grains on her wet fingertips.

"Pica," she repeats. "Theh's something wrong with me."

"The soap?"

"Ah jes crave it. I thank it's a deficiency…. You know, if you cahn't git what you need nat-ural-ly, you go about the wrong places for gittin it…"

Yeah.

"So, would you like to grab a cup of coffee? You could wash the soap out of your mouth. There's a diner down the…" I stop myself. There's someone on the other end of that ring in the bluing. He isn't one for messing with.

"I'm sorry," I sputter. "You don't know me and… And I'm sure you need to finish your washing and go home."

She white-knuckle wrings a shirt over the industrial sink and pink water bleeds out. "Pete," she looks me in the eye. "Ah am nawt goin' back."

The water is pink and the laundry suds are pink and the dryer windows have a faint pink film. And for a moment, it's as if I'm seeing the launderette through rose-colored lenses. I take a step closer to her, but the plastic laundry basket still separates us. When I kick it to the side, the hammer topples out. Its claw is still sticky with brain and blood, bits of bone.

All I can think is that she's safe now.

I take a tee-shirt and wipe a few burgundy speckles from her cheek. "Let me buy you a cup of coffee for the road," I say.

I have this deficiency. And when you're missing something naturally, you tend to fill it with something that isn't good for you at all.

Disparate Temperatures

In 1906, a lifeguard patrols the extravagant Sutro Baths by rowboat, and there's only one swimmer he's come to watch.

Fidelia, he thought as he paid his dime. *Fidelia*, he thought for seven miles as the Southern Pacific jostled its way. *Fidelia*, he thought as the streetcar deposited him and a horde of reveling youth at the oceanside park. The swimmers ran with mad folly toward the Baths. Below the labyrinthine structure, waves crashed in thunderous applause, wild lilies bloomed, and cliff-lodged cypress trees reached to the sea. Teddy breathed in the lilies and the salt and the faint odor of brass polish all at once, and allowed himself to think of Fidelia once again.

When Fidelia's lovely little face came into his mind's eye, it was if someone had smacked him straight in the heart with a flyswatter. A bracing sting of sorts. It didn't crush his heart, exactly, but captured it under the metal mesh with singular precision. A few years before, Teddy had taken a quarter from his mother's jar to join his friends at the pools. And, to be fair, upon realizing that Saturdays were free for children, he attempted to return the coin. But, his mother interceded with her newly-purchased flyswatter from Montgomery Co. She had smacked his thieving little hand until it welted.

He was no longer a child. He pulled on the sweater which identified his duty and boarded the rowboat to begin his shift. Unlike the 10,000 swimmers required to wear suits provided by the establishment – black wool or, if well-laundered grey, with SUTRO BATHS knitted in white block letters – Teddy sported checkered slacks and LIFEGUARD.

The Baths were just shy of 500 feet in length, and more than 250 feet wide. The rowboat was a matter of practicality. The swimmers bounded into the water by trampolines, flying rings, slides, swings, toboggan slides, and diving platforms. In the cacophony, Teddy bobbed silently. He maintained austere composure as he considered both the great importance and absolute futility of his job. He was but a single signpost warning of the possibility of getting drowned.

Still, there was no better sea bathing in the world. "Rival in magnitude, utility and beauty, the famous abluvion resorts of Titus, Caracalla, Nero or Diocletian..." read the programme. Indeed, there were noble pavilions, balustrades, promenades, alcoves, and corridors adorned with fountains, tropical flowers, and the collected treasure of foreign travels, all leading to the pools themselves. Unheated seawater filled a great plunge tank. There were seven more heated to varying temperatures, ten-degree gaps between each, from ice-cold to a steaming ninety degrees.

A roof of 100,000 glass panes allowed the sunlight to break across the swimmers. And in that shimmering melee of thousands of dark bathing costumes in millions of gallons of sea, he saw Fidelia. He recognized the elegant line of her pale neck against the wet wool. Teddy knew the curve of her calf and the steam-curls of her hair, new since their childhood. He knew the perfect arch of her foot as she emerged from the toboggan slide. And, floating yards and yards away, he knew that when she dove into the seawater tank it would be one fluid movement, neither sound nor splash.

But he was mistaken. Fidelia made a comic leap, arms and legs whirling akimbo, in a very wet and indecorous performance.

Teddy was stricken. Either this was not Fidelia, and how could he not recognize *his* Fidelia, or there was some terrible abluvion of the Fidelia he'd ever known.

Teddy steadied himself on the little boat and paddled closer to the saltwater pool. He watched Fidelia as she climbed the stairs to the waterwheel and laid down on it. The giant wheel slowly revolved, dumping tangles of swimmers into the pool. As Fidelia was discarded into the water, she crashed screaming into a rowdy mess of boys. She threw her head back in a fit of giggles.

Teddy's heart was no longer trapped under the fine mesh of the swatter. Instead, its beating seemed to seize. There was cutting sensation as if he had dived into the hot pool, climbed out, raced down to the small ice-cold pool, and dove in there.

Teddy straightened his back and embraced the gallantry of his lifeguard sweater. "You there," he addressed the girl, "be careful." He broke out his most manly timber, "You mustn't play so roughly with children about."

The girl simply laughed and shook her curls.

Fidelia, he thought for the very last time. *Fidelia, I hope that you're waiting for a locker attendant for hours, cold and shivering, miserable, in your rented wool bathing suit.*

Duck, Duck, Goose

The games we play.

First, you get oh-so-pretty for the party. Do whatever primping rites you do. Then, when you arrive, you must be fresh and cheerful and willing to play. Everybody forms constellations, and you don't want to be left out. It seems like it's a very long time before it's your turn. They go up and down and around and around. Over and over.

When you're finally It, the show is all yours. You keep the cocktail balanced while exchanging charming observations. You run fingers through someone's hair. *Is he the one? No.* You brush a bit of canapé off another's tie. *Is he the one? No.* You accept triple air kisses from another. *Is he the one? No.* Touch his shoulder, look in his eye, practice a smile. *No, no, no.*

And then, there's one who is of a different feather. He's charming. He thinks you're charming. He looks like that actor/singer/athlete/other that you had a crush on when you were fifteen. He's artistic enough to be interesting, but ambitious enough to be viable. And you're relieved to discover that he's not gay.

You tell your best cocktail party anecdote. His hand will touch yours when he brings you a fresh drink. Then, you will find some innocuous but necessary reason for him to talk to you again soon. To be certain, he will leave with your email address, mobile phone number, IM handle, land line, home and vacation addresses, and contact information at work.

Once you are home, you may drink a bit and text him pictures you take in the bathtub with your cell phone.

After that, he will want to spend some time with you.

When you are not going out with him, you will stalk him through his friends, your friends, Facebook, LinkedIn, Twitter, Google Alerts, and perhaps even genotype a strand of his hair to ensure that he's not interested in anyone else. Then, with all of the information you know about him, you will be able to surprise him with all of the things that you happen to have in common.

You will cook him something wonderful, perhaps only wearing an apron. You will find the action figure he never got from Santa. You will be coiffed and lipsticked and never wear granny panties. You will smile and be obliging, even when the things he wants to do are so horribly lame.

And he will begin to like you for this. He may even love you for it. At which point, you will begin to find him terribly boring. You will unceremoniously dump him in the mush pot. Then, you will take your seat, cross your ankles, and wait. If you are patient, you will be tapped on the shoulder. And the chase will begin again.

Flightless Birds

A farmer's wife has dreams of a more delicious life.

Sunday supper was the same as Sunday breakfast: chicken fried chicken and biscuits with sawmill gravy. Monday supper was livers and gizzards with turnip or collard greens. Tuesday was chicken and dumplings (Aunt Pearl's recipe). Wednesday was homestyle-fried, dredged in buttermilk and crushed Kellogg's corn flakes. Thursday was butter-baked chicken with okra or string beans (fresh in season, otherwise pickled from the pantry). Friday was chicken pot pie, except when it wasn't. Claire went to the Ladies Auxiliary dinner at the VFW once a month and they went to the fish fry at Saint Anne's during Lent, too. Saturday was leftovers.

Claire and Albert both woke to the rooster. And so, with the exception of some chicory coffee, breakfast had to wait until chores were done and the rest of the farm was fed. It was late enough and hearty enough to hold their hunger until supper. Depending on the day of the week, breakfast was over easy, sunny side up, scrambled, poached, coaxed into a soufflé, carefully cracked to make eggs-in-the-basket, or coddled in porcelain cups. There were creamy grits, biscuits, apple butter and jam. On days that Claire was fortunate enough to serve a thick slice of ham, there was also redeye gravy.

Claire was a fine cook made better by the quality of her ingredients. The Rhode Island Reds were free range birds and their eggs were too large to fit in a standard carton. Albert had to special-order oversized crates from King's supply. The yolks were creamy and as yellow as the buttercups in Claire's childhood. Hold the buttercup under your chin, her sisters would tease, if it reflects yellow, it means that you like boys.

She had liked one boy and that was enough. Albert was as docile, quiet and friendly as the birds. He was gentle to the brown-striped chicks in their warmers, yet an efficient dispatcher of the less-productive hens. The temperature had dropped below freezing several times that winter and the good layers had become less so. The seven pound hens kept them well-fed.

Though she was too polite to say so, Claire didn't much care for the other ladies at the VFW. She went for the food: chafing dishes of pot roast or beef brisket or spiral sliced ham. Buffet-style, take as much as you like. And so, when the February dinner turned out to be chicken à la king, she quietly put on her coat and left the hall.

Claire sat in the truck and considered her options. She felt the delicious freedom at the thought of three hours of her own. After the truck warmed up, she headed to town.

The restaurant was one of only seventeen of its kind in the country. It was profiled on public radio. The neon sign blinked, tossing colors onto the snow at her feet.

Claire checked the amount of cash in her wallet, touched up her lipstick, and entered.

It was a jewel-box of a place. Perhaps eight tables of sophisticated diners in cashmere turtlenecks and twinsets. Claire didn't try to pronounce the dishes, but simply pointed at the menu, reassured by the waiter's effusive agreement. The boxes were elegantly arranged, the offerings as bright and delicate as her other's brooches: an eel napoleon of fried tofu, crispy won-ton, mashed eel, pumpkin and ginger; yellowtail steak with baby bok choy, enoki mushroom and sake; uni marinated in coconut milk; negitoro roll plump with fatty tuna and scallion; and a petite salad of sliced sashimi, hearts of palm, plum caviar, and lotus root. Claire ate it all. Her cheeks bloomed more fervently with each tingling bite. And when she was finally satiated, she asked to thank the chef.

Her waiter escorted her to the kitchen—the counters so clean, the aromas so foreign from her own—and assured her the chef spoke very fine English.

"Oh, thank you," she effused. And then she started to cry. She told him about the farm and the hens, about Albert and about the 350 days of chicken suppers each year. She talked more than she had in quite some time. And then, just as she began to doubt that his English was indeed very fine, he clasped her hands.

"Special ingredient," he said.

The chef motioned to a metal box the size and shape of a Quaker Oats canister. He placed a little brass key in her palm. She smiled gratefully and made the long drive home to Albert.

Despite her competence in the kitchen, leftover gizzards did not fare especially well. They were chewy when hot, and positively squeaked when cold. Claire tried to season them with a bit of paprika plus corn relish on the side. She took the key from her pocket and unlocked the box. She didn't dare cook the secret ingredient, lest it lose its special flavor. She simply rolled it in cornmeal and plated it with the gizzards and a sprig of parsley.

Albert sighed happily as he sat down to supper. "Well, dear, the weather seems to be turning for us. Our Reds will have us rich in big brown eggs again soon. It's going to be a good..."

Year, he would have said. It's going to be a good year. Except he didn't. He stopped in the middle of his sentence and collapsed on the kitchen floor. Claire wiped the kitchen counter, took her keys, and closed the door behind her.

In the truck, she searched the dial for the station that kept her company so many plucking afternoons. *Oh, public radio is just so wonderful. How lovely to be connected to the rest of the world.* A great white expanse of snow lay glistening on the road ahead.

For instance, she thought, *the liver of the tiger blowfish, or fugu, is 1,200 times more deadly than cyanide. And there are only seventeen chefs in America licensed to use the fugu hiki to cut it out.*

The Gold Rush Widow

A dam at the middle fork of the Yuba River separates husband and wife during California's hydraulic mining era.

William Henry Green had not been dead. At least, Eliza Jane assumed as much during their long separations. And, if he had passed, she had not been so informed. This was unfortunate, as Eliza had a pretty pale cameo of a face and hair the color of corn silk. She would have looked absolutely lovely in widow's black. She was a modest woman, perhaps more humble than modest, but even she knew she was best in black. William Henry had once made her a present of a black velvet gown with a spray of lace at the throat from his first profit. The rest he'd invested with seven other men in an auspicious parcel on the other side of the Yuba River. And she'd only seen him twice since.

Unlike most other prospectors who had traversed the prairie to seek their families' fortunes, the Greens had found a bantam streak of gold on the edge of their own land. William wove Eliza Jane promises of social prominence in San Francisco before he left to search for more gold at French Corral. The velvet dress stayed in the hope chest with the wedding china she didn't see the sense in using alone and the baby things which she sensed may never be used at all.

Eliza Jane worked the small farm on her own, sending her goods to the market or camps with her Chinese neighbors. William blasted black powder at hillsides with a boy's enthusiasm, hoping to unearth buried gold. He was more than a man with a pick and pan. He had a complicated operation of sluice boxes, ditches, flues, and toms in play. She saw the effects of his work in the mining debris that clogged the water between them. The river swelled, rising above its bank and encroaching the town with gravel and muck. The slickens buried fences downstream and choked the fruit trees.

The foothill miners and the valley farmers would've nearly killed each other if not for the dam. Stretching 400 feet across the river, the English Dam retained a reservoir two-and-a-half miles back. It was built of timber, stacked in the style of a log cabin, a shored up with stone fill and the pressure of 650 million cubic feet of water. The surrounding land was cratered and treeless, the noise was still terrible, and the towns were crowded with stinking saloons. But the dam kept most of the silt and slick from harming the peach crop and washing the streets in mud.

Eliza Jane had seen William once outside the dry goods store. Though he was the one who'd grown bearded and sun-burnt, it was he who did not appear to recognize her. They exchanged the awkward pleasantries of mere acquaintances. Yet, before they parted to their own horses, he kissed her on the cheek and she could feel the strange burr of his whiskers, his breath hot on her ear. They left each other without tears or ceremony. Eliza Jane hated the gray ramble of town. Even the church was coated in dirt.

The second time she saw William was in their home a few days later. She had come in from the orchards, hat in hand, and he was sitting at the kitchen table eating marmalade from the jar. He'd washed and shaven and put on clean trousers. Wordlessly, they climbed under the cool bedsheets. And he'd left in the pre-dawn morning just as quietly as he'd came.

Eliza Jane, asleep during this departure, was rattled awake at five. In her fugue state, she found it hard to determine whether William had actually been there, much less that he was already gone. She stepped onto the porch in her nightdress and felt dizzy and chilled. The world smelled different.

And then, just as the flood surged the farm, did she realize that the dam had let go.

A wave nearly one hundred feet high submerged the farmhouse. The rushing water carried a cargo of trees, rocks, brush, and chemicals from the mines. As the water turned a bend, the debris became lodged, forming a nearly hundred foot high barrier, seemingly a dam of its own design, which saved some of the downstream towns from being destroyed by the crash of rubble.

Down at the crossing, a stagecoach traversed the covered bridge over the Yuba. The passengers marveled at the divine intercession which must have saved them as the debris barricade broke and the flood swept away the place they had just passed.

As Eliza Jane was enveloped into the surge, she could see the bridge lifted off its supports and carried upstream. She sputtered and tried to swim for the hope chest as it floated and flipped and abandoned its cargo with a fierce lack of sentimentality. William's bow tie, which would never be worn in an opera box in the city, passed through her fingers. The velvet gown tangled around her like an unwelcome advance and then floated away. A tiny christening gown swirled around a teapot and then both were lost.

Eliza Jane closed her eyes. She imagined the flood washing over the town's dirty clapboard hotel, the broom factory, and the blacksmith's. She could see the water rushing through hundreds of barns as it was now her own. She imagined the land clean and green, sweet again in spring. And she yielded herself peacefully to the baptism of the flood.

The Gulf of Aden

A cruise ship is attacked by pirates to the mild inconvenience of its passengers.

Sugar was freckling in the sun. Even after two weeks at sea, she still didn't resemble her bronzed shipmates. They were uniformly tanned, drawn taut, bleached, waxed, capped, and shellacked. Their bodies made unnatural angles as their linen shirts and dresses billowed in the breeze. Sugar wore the requisite oversized sunglasses of their class. With her name, she could be one of them. Cricket, Tinsley, Muffy, Sugar. It was either a socialite's name or a stripper's. You just had to take the context clues. She had never been able to live up to one or down to the other until recently.

But, there she stood on the lido deck of the Silver Slipper, pale and spangled in a confection of a dress. It was lovely, really: one-shoulder, bias-cut silk chiffon in layers of creamy jade and celadon. It was one of 23 she'd bought especially for the voyage. She knew quality; she read her magazines. And though she wasn't afflicted with that match-matchy taste of a poor girl going to prom, she hadn't mastered casual wear. That is, she hadn't yet perfected the art of looking casual in terribly expensive clothes. There was sort of a carelessness in the way the others dressed, as if a cruise was an everyday affair.

She leaned on the railing, drink in hand, eavesdropping. The passengers talked about other drinks, other cruises, other ports. They told the same stories over and again, sometimes to the same people, about mildly mortifying incidents that always turned out all right in the end. From Deck 10, she could see for miles. The skies were clear, the sea was calm, and the warm weather rivaled that of the Caribbean. There was little to look at except a few seabirds. Every now and again, the small boats of day fisherman from Oman and Yemen came into view.

Two white skiffs appeared. The fishermen waved their arms with such fortitude that Sugar almost put decorum aside to wave back. One of the men lifted something much larger than a net handle or pole up to his shoulder and aimed. The warhead careened towards the Silver Slipper and exploded in the observation lounge. White phosphorus smoke streamed from the bridge. The man raised the grenade launcher again, and Sugar flattened herself against the deck. She could see the propulsive trail and hear the second shot punching through layers of metal.

The Slipper zigzagged sharply to escape the attack. It had been travelling fast, traversing the Gulf at nearly 20 knots. The evasive maneuvers sent the pool water crashing over the deck. Before the passengers could fathom their wetness, they heard the terrible symphony of bottles and stemware falling from the open shelves in the bar. Surviving liqueurs rolled through the debris and collected under the very wet and entangled lounge chairs on Deck 10.

The drenched passengers, Sugar included, made their way to the inner compartments. When asked about the risk of piracy at the start of their two-day, 491-mile passage through the Gulf of Aden, the captain had said there was no need for an abundance of caution. The ship is fast, the decks are high, there are so many people on board... it's not an attractive target, he'd assured.

And, here they were, somewhere between Safaga and Oman. The pirates had somehow scaled the four stories up to the promenade. They were darker than the passengers—the color and shine of cherry cola. And, they were armed with automatic weapons. Shouting and gesturing, they corralled passengers into the ballroom. The crew was forced to abandon their stations and join the rest. The group was unusually quiet, observing the pirates as if attending a play or musical revue. They rustled a bit, though, in the discomfort of minor scrapes and wet clothing which was becoming cold.

Sugar arranged the damp layers of fabric under her bottom. The rustle of silk chiffon caught the notice of one of the patrolling pirates. He gave Sugar the once-over, then took her hand with an eye to her ring. She drew back out of reflex. And he, out of pirate reflex, slammed the butt of his gun into her nose. Blood spattered across the chiffon. The dress resembled nothing more than a puddle of melted mint chip ice cream. Sugar tore a strip of fabric from the hem and used it to staunch the bleeding. She knew how to take a punch.

The assaulter argued in Somali, or perhaps Arabic, with a fellow pirate. From what Sugar could determine, they weren't aboard for jewelry or 22 clean, candy-colored dresses. There was much more reward in ransom, given the number of passengers and their collective offshore wealth. If you damage the product too much, you don't get any money.

She had only wanted a little adventure.

When Peter died, there was a bit of insurance money. While she would never have wished for the accident, there was a certain relief in the absence of her husband. It had been a horrible marriage. And, before and instead of dealing with his debts, Sugar simply booked passage on the Silver Slipper. They had no children and no pets. They had no savings. She gave notice on their rented flat in Effingham and donated the furniture and such to the children's receiving home. She had bought steamer trunks and a new wardrobe, boarded the train in Surrey, and didn't look back.

From the port in Southampton, she'd sailed through the Atlantic, the Straight of Gibraltar, the Mediterranean, the Suez Canal, and the Red Sea. It had, up to the Somali pirates, been a pleasant, peaceful, and delicious journey. There had been ports of call of indescribable color and beauty in Lisbon, Civitavecchia, and Luxor. On land and sea, there had been the most fabulous food. In fact, between their dramas, the pirates were enjoying slices of foie gras terrine with port wine jelly and white truffle oil on toasted brioche from the buffet.

There was a sound like the wick-wick-wick of eggbeaters. A pirate rushed into the ballroom, sweating, and the sound became louder, a sort of steady chopping. They conferred passionately amongst themselves, alternately pointing to the captain and pointing up. Then, they left as quickly as they'd come. They took some profiteroles and a jar of sturgeon roe. Otherwise, they commandeered neither hostages nor treasure.

Apparently, in such situations, a navy-scrambled helicopter can be overhead in as few as 15 minutes.

Within a few days, things were back in their proper places. The ship's doctor taped Sugar's nose. Both her eyes were black, but the bridge of her nose was still too tender to the touch to support sunglasses. She rested on a newly-clean deck chair, eyes closed, listening to the cocktail banter. They talked about how the broken glass and pool water had damaged their leather-soled shoes. How dirty the pirates' fingernails were, how tacky it was for them to have taken the jar of Sevruga caviar. The inconvenience of having the observation area closed for repairs. They talked about other cocktail parties to come, long after they'd disembarked, at which they could tell their friends they'd encountered real pirates in the Gulf of Aden. And, as one noted between sips, how unfortunate it was that he wasn't roughed up like the woman in green, because the retelling would be so much more interesting.

The cruise line, it seems, was offering restitution for the inconvenience of the piracy by way of additional complimentary days of travel. The passengers discussed whether that was tacky, too. For her part, Sugar would stay aboard the Slipper for another 81 days until it returned to Southampton. Or not. By the time they'd approached Dubai, she only had £81 and a handful of foreign coins left. It would be a relief when the money was gone.

Hearts and Sleeves

*During the Cold War, a talented magician
teaches his techniques to CIA operatives.*

The man with the remarkable mustache had been waiting in the dark for a long time. But not as long as the others. When viewed in a properly-lit room, the mustache was indeed impressive: silver and lustrous as an arctic fox tail, curling in perfect symmetry at the edges. It was one of a collection.

There, in the dark, he felt a rough electricity. It was a nervous anticipation he hadn't felt since childhood, when he'd first performed the Torn and Restored trick and was quite unsure whether the pieces of the playing card would come back together.

His story was Dickensian. At age eleven, having only ever been called "Boy," he'd chosen the name King Fields for himself. The moniker was inspired by advertisement painted on the east side of the barn: a winsome brunette holding a king-size pack of Chesterfield cigarettes. In the shade of that barn, King practiced with a Svengali deck he'd palmed from the five-and-dime. He worked the tricks over and again until they were clean. And, when he was ready, the boy packed his practical magic and hopped a freight train. Unlike some other young buskers in the city, King wasn't a con. He had a good act and he got good tips in his hat. King was much like his Ambitious Card trick, wherein the selected card continually rises to the top after being placed in the middle of the deck.

And so, through luck and circumstance, he rose to become *King Fields - Master of Deception.* His shows were advertised everywhere from bright marquees to barn sides. And his matchless talent as a magician was what gained the attention of the Company.

The project was Flash Classified. His handlers briefed him on the Air America flight to the Farm. They'd played to his vanity and they'd played to his patriotism, but they needn't have. King wanted the job. He appreciated the opportunity to apply to magic to the great machinations of the real world.

The Company first contracted him to create an instruction manual. "The purpose of this book," the handler had said, "is to instruct the reader so he may learn to perform a variety of acts secretly and undetectably."

King drafted a manuscript concerning the application of the magician's technique to covert delivery of materials, misleading movements to cover normally prohibited activities, influence of the perceptions of other persons, various forms of disguise, and secret signaling systems. The book was published for exclusive distribution under the title *Some Practical Applications of the Art of Prestidigitation.* If found in an agent's possession, it would resemble nothing more than a hobbyist's how-to guide. But under the top-hatted cover hid countless secrets of value a professional in clandestine operations.

After completion of the tactical manual, he was tapped to both teach operatives at the Farm and to research new deceptive techniques and materials. King's savoir-faire aided agents in the field to perform dangerous, provocative, and even lethal acts.

As King was teaching CIA operatives to surreptitiously dispatch pills and poisons, mind-altering chemicals, and biological weapons, he realized that the strategies did not often fit the needs of female agents. The gentler sex required their own rulebook when it came to disorienting, discrediting, injuring, and terminating targets. He proposed sleights of hand fitting smaller gloves.

Ardita, a lovely operative he privately regarded as prettier than the Chesterfields' girl, explained the difference. A male colleague, she noted, could hide arsenic in the hollowed end of a pencil and deliver the poison as easily as making a sketch. But, a woman would need two identical pencils, one poison and one plain, as a man would be sure to take one from her to amend anything she might sketch herself.

But I wouldn't change a thing about you, King had thought. *Ar-di-ta, fresh and bright and tart as a lemon.*

That was a long time ago. And now Ardita was gone, other good agents, too. The mission to Moscow had failed miserably. And whether or not he believed it, the Company blamed the compromise on his defective magic.

He wasn't a spook, but he wasn't a civilian either. Thanks to his replete selection of mustaches, spectacles, prostheses, and tints, was no longer recognized as a famed prestidigitator. His 201 file had been destroyed. He was less than expendable, he was disavowed. King was nothing more than a ghost.

There, in the black hallway, the newly-mustachioed magician prepared to complete his self-appointed mission. He heard the elevator doors open and his target emerge, cursing the super for what he believed to be a blown bulb. The mark struggled with his keys. The magician closed in. As the door swung open to the dark apartment, the magician's hand rose with intention. Before he could act, the room was filled with light and laughter.

"Surprise!" shouted thirty or so well-dressed strangers. "Happy Birthday, Ivan!"

King dropped his arm to his side, silently released the weapon and concealed it under his left shoe. After a moment of disconcert, he realized that Ivan's enthusiastic friends had been waiting in the dark on the inside of the door, at least a few minutes longer than he'd been waiting outside, and certainly with more cheerful intentions.

A good performer is always adaptable. Instead of slinking away from the party, King plastered on a showman's smile and pretended to be the evening's hired entertainment. He had nothing left to lose.

He started with some of his close-up specialties – coin and card and chop cup effects – his patter directing the guests' attentions where he could have the best angles. He then made a few acts of transposition wherein cocktails changed places to the astonishment of their drinkers. After which, in a bit he called "Haunted Hank," he levitated his foulard and made it dance around as if it was possessed by a spirit. To prove that there was no gimmick, he took Ivan's handkerchief and did the trick again. The tiny spirit floated over the punchbowl with unseen manipulation.

Ivan was impressed. He inquired of his friends, but none admitted to hiring the entertainer or even knowing his name. Ivan approached the magician and asked for his card. With a flourish, a pencil was produced, and the magician drew a looping, illegible signature on a paper cocktail napkin. The guest of honor took his next drink, swayed, and fell.

The magician exited the party. As he crossed the still-dark hall, he considered the illusions necessary in his disappearance to come. *Disappearing is the easy part*, King told himself. And, with a final thought to his unspoken affection for Ardita, he conceded, *The hardest trick is to really be seen.*

A Noise that Doesn't Stop

A phantom train beckons.

The train labors from two until four. Then rests until 4:15. The train labors from 4:15 until 6 or 6:30, maybe, but by then she doesn't pretend to sleep. The house is gabled, with the upstairs one long room with a crank-style window at each end. The room's only good for standing in the middle, so mostly it's the bedroom, which requires less standing around. At two the sound begins, not changing much if it seeps through the cracks or pushes waves against the panes. The steam exhales with a squeal, the engine throbs a bass cardiac beat, and instead of screeching on the tracks, as you might expect, the wheels say hush-hush-HUSH-hush down the line. What was a whistle is now more of a hum. The first night, exhausted from cleaning, she was deep asleep when the whistle blew. Olive went flying out of bed and smacked her head on the slanted ceiling. Hurt and confused, she puddled onto the floor and cried as the train lumbered on.

The house is perfect for one. Quite good for two, but only if they really liked each other. Downstairs holds a living area, empty as of yet, with red lacquer floor. It opens onto a concrete porch, stained in places, dripping in vines. The roof is covered in ivy, which sometimes pushes its way through the shingles and into the house. Most mornings, Olive can hear the squirrels scamper the length of the roof and take a flying leap into the lone peach tree. *Why red lacquer?* she wonders. Maybe they wanted to bring some city sophistication here. Maybe an artist in a mad fit was so inspired. Maybe it's not lacquer at all. She thinks about possible uses for a red-floored room when the train keeps her up nights, but by the morning she really can't remember any.

The bathroom is small. Everything is, actually, but it doesn't feel so bad. It's like being a guest in a very eccentric hotel – single serving soap, one set of towels, shower but no tub. There's a basement, too, into which Olive hasn't ventured. Her favorite room is the kitchen. Though she only changed the yellowed Battenberg curtains and replenishes pitchers of wildflowers, it seems much brighter. Someone had tacked butchers' paper over the kitchen walls and covered them in hand-drawn maps. In pencil and watercolor, hundred of little islands and peninsulas, replete with lighthouses, pepper the walls. At first glance it appears to be the Eastern seaboard, but upon closer inspection the penciled names of the coves and such are unfamiliar. And that's it – that's the whole house.

Rent is cheap. Two seventy-five a month, all utilities paid. They wanted to keep the house in the family, but are fine to rent it for now. They cautioned her about not having a tub. They cautioned her that the stench of the barn carries over acres on breezy days. It's the wheat and milo she smells mostly. Warm and hop-full like a drafted beer. No one said anything about the train.

The other night it made a new sound. In the quiet space

between 4:00 and 4:15, it sustained a pretty hum. Mmmmm, just like the alto section warming up. Then hush-hush it chugged again. It was light out when the train had passed. It was 6:47.

The train had passed, she thought. That can't be right. After four months of fitful nights she realized: a train can't just go on by for two-and-a-half hours. Unless it's a very long train, of course. Or a very slow train. Or many trains, one directly after the other.

In July, the train came at 11:30. It had been coming a little earlier, sustaining a little later, just by a few minutes, but still... This was early. She sensed its growing impatience. Sometimes Olive dreamed of a cranberry-colored knapsack, tied to a stick hobo-style. She didn't really have anything of sentiment to fill it with, but perhaps it was empty, just waiting to be filled. She dreamed of racing through the milo at night, fearless of the electricity of crickets, running for the boxcars. How far can you go? Nestled on a bag of grain to protect from bumpy tracks, the open car door a picture-window to the world: past farms and fields, changing plains of color, towards verdant valleys, through dark clusters of trees whose roots clawed for earth but only curled over eroding hillsides. To the salt in the middle of the sky and the sea.

The sun sets late in the summer. Almost ten. She had wheeled a galvanized trough to the porch and filled it halfway with the hose. The rest she added pot by pot from the stove. The rust rings on the porch matched the makeshift bath. In another time it was used to ice bottled beer. When the farm had flourished, they told her, the extra hands had slept here. The porch was a summer kitchen. Olive envied those impervious workers who celebrated a hard day with hard drinking. Waking up the next morning to do it again. She stepped out of her sundress and pretzeled into the tub, stirring her knees to mix the disparate temperatures. A bath becomes a luxury in a dry state.

She should bathe in the day, really. The sun could warm the water and save the boiling. There was no need for modesty with the limited visitors. Jeremy couriered a portion of groceries and bottled milk from the main house's delivery every Monday. Sometimes she would see Jeremy or Justin on the threshers, but it was too distant to tell which was which. At night, veiled by ivy anyhow, she could let her skin drink up. Add mint from the garden and it smells like a julep, add juniper and it could be gin. Time passed quickly waiting for the train.

As soon as night fell, you could hear it coming. Panting ah-ah-aah like a woman in the throes, and the whistle her relief. Light bathed the fields in amber and gold and bottle green, making those dry grains brilliant again. Time suspended. It was light out when the train finally passed. Late enough to burn off the haze and let the sky stretch in impeccable blue, but the water was still warm.

By August the train couldn't wait for night. It sustained late into the morning and started early in the evening, inching in on both sides until it was ceaseless sound. When Jeremy dropped by with sundries and a rum cake from his wife, she'd asked him about the train.

The noise must bother you, running so close to the house, she had said. *Maybe you just take it for granted, like the smell of grain or the dry heat.*

Jeremy considered for a moment. *You can borrow the truck if you need to, Olive*, he offered, but then he backed off the porch, puzzled, forgetting to leave the cake.

The noise didn't stop. Like a pilgrim repeating the Jesus prayer, the train fervently repeated its mantra. Olive unclipped the kitchen curtain and smoothed it out. Peppermint soap, an extra dress, toothbrush, comb, a small paper bag of peaches, an envelope of money, bottles of water, and a leather journal with photos pressed between the pages. She traced his face with her fingers and kissed an apology on the picture of John and their towheaded boy. *I tried to stop*, she whispered. *Honestly, I tried.*

Olive tied the bundle with kitchen twine, leaving two long loops to lasso over her shoulder. She rushed past the chittering squirrels, the buzz of the thresher. She rushed through the scratches of brambles and chiggers and milkweed silk. It was certain that through acres of grain she'd finally see her train. Oh, to be away from this place and away from that city too. My train runs to the coast. It never stops.

I tried to stop, she panted, *but I was just too thirsty here.*

Phoning Arcadia

A telephone operator's mistake creates a romantic connection for two strangers.

The first thing that they tell you is that you absolutely must not listen in. Of course, that's the first rule you break. You've got to make sure they're connected at first, and then you've got to make sure the line is clear before you disconnect. You're bound to hear both swell and lousy stuff in the process. And, the more swell or lousy it is, the more you have to find out what happens next. It's my first week, and the girls have already shown me how to make two sharp raps of my pencil against the desk so the caller thinks I've switched off.

Working at the Plaza, there's always something sensational going through the boards: calls too early or too late, calls to women who aren't their wives, calls to florists to make good. It's better than any paperback romance.

We're all unmarried and some of us are nearing 25. We really shouldn't giggle about these terribly tacky conversations; we're certainly more desperate ourselves.

Just this morning, though, Miss Lily in 208 had me patch her through to the Arcade. It wasn't even the breakfast hour. Even I know better than to call a man while he's still sleeping off the night before.

When I turned the key to connect, the other operator said, "Whadya want?"

"Miss Lillian Dash for room 103, please."

"Oh, ain't you a polite one. This ain't the Ritz, honey. I'll see if he'll come down to the phone."

Now, I knew then that something wasn't quite right. I flipped up both keys but stayed on.

"Hullo?"

"You darling, darling man!" cooed Miss Lily. "I know I should have waited for you to call me, but I just couldn't wait!" Everything Miss Lily said was an exclamation.

"Who is this?"

"Oh, you card! Dance the night away with a girl and pretend you don't know. Why of all the sweet nothings we whispered into each other's ears, I could tell your voice anywhere.... I simply can't wait until tonight to see you! Did you get a coffee pot and a shave yet?"

"I've got five cents set aside for a bottomless cup. That should wake me."

"Didn't you sleep well, darling? After all those Manhattans, I think you'd be sound as a baby. Oh, I did call too early, didn't

I?"

"No, ma'am, it's just that with the thin walls and chicken wire ceilings, it's pretty hard to nod off around here. The bed linens are clean and it's only 50 cents a night, so it's better than most on this row."

"Ma'am! Dear, you're a crack-up! Calling me ma'am after you've seen my rouged knees! And, if you don't care for the Arcade, check in to the Plaza with me .... Oh, that was a little fresh, wasn't it? Check into the Astor or the Grand, then."

I realized my mistake, and bit my lip to keep an audible gasp from the line. The gentleman wasn't at the Arcade on 35th Street. He was at the Arcade on the Bowery. I'd read in *The New Yorker* that uptown hotels like the Majestic, the Savoy, the Nassau, and the Astor had supplied the names of downtown lodgings, much to the dismay of the hoteliers. Of all the arcades to which I could have misdirected Miss Lily's call—a shopping arcade, a shooting gallery, penny amusements, or even a dirty-pictures show—I had routed her to a Bowery flophouse.

"I think you may have the wrong man."

"I'm certain you're the right one. Don't be so modest! You were the best dancer in that gin joint, and you must let me show you off to that frightful Millicent tonight. She's always going on and on about her beau. Well, darling, she'll just crumple when she sees how handsome you are."

"I'm not who you think I am."

"Ooh, how mysterious! Well, dear, I'm sure I'll see more of your secret side after a few more highballs."

"I appreciate the invitation, it's just …. well, I've got to go wash plates and coffee pots at Horn & Hardart's tonight to earn some flop money. It was nice to make your acquaintance."

"You stop your teasing. I'm off to buy a lovely green number to match those eyes you said you adored. Perhaps it would be nice to live in a little coldwater flat for a while instead of just ribbing about it. It's simply too exhausting getting marcelled and manicured, going to all these parties, having to be gay all the time. Oh, imagine that: me peeling potatoes and hanging laundry in an apron and bare feet!"

"In my experience, ma'am, it only takes a few pennies to unlock life's charm. And a hard day's work is the best way to sleep sound."

Miss Lily cracked up. "You sound so adorably earnest when

you talk like that. I'll just split the sides of my dressing gown if I laugh any harder. Now, go drink some hair o' the dog and get your shoes shined. You can pick me up at nine."

"Yes, ma'am," the man said quietly. And when Miss Lily had finally abandoned the line, I heard him whisper, "What in the fresh hell was that all about?"

I let out a chirp of laughter.

"Is someone on the line?"

I turned the key and ended the call.

So, at the end of my shift, I'll smooth the dents from the headset out of my hairdo and apply fresh lip rouge. I'll put on my green coat with the badger cuffs and my yellow hat. Then I'll hoof it past the hotels and peep shows to Horn & Hardart's automat. I've got a nickel for a French-drip and a dime for dessert. If I'm lucky, I'll look through the pie windows and see a certain someone washing dishes. I think I can catch his eye. I'm almost 23, after all. It's about time I met a gentleman.

ScentEasy

*A visit to an environmentally-friendly perfumery
makes a girl lonely for her old life.*

Tucked between the vegan bakery and the outsider art gallery is a space as clean as vapor. The glass is immaculate. From the sidewalk, you can see deep into the shop. Row follows row of milk-glass shelves and repeating bottles, like a kaleidoscope that's lost its color. I think I'm the kind of girl who shops here now.

Dalton's new girlfriend is thin, brunette, and childishly earnest. She's nothing like me at all. Though, this morning I went to Aveda for a cut and color (warm hazelnut, nice, I guess) and a toluene-free mani-pedi. And, I picked up a new pullover. It's plain and painfully expensive. You know that boutique where the sweaters are displayed one-by-one like pastries in a case? Except more serious? So it's nice. Made from bamboo or made locally or something. I don't think bamboo grows here, so it has to be one or the other, not both.

You know, when the President said he had a sense of hopefulness about this new green market, and that this investment in clean energy will produce real benefits for the American economy, I think things may have gotten carried away. I know people get excited whenever he uses the word hope.... but things just got so much greener overnight. Everybody looked for tax credits and subsidies, not just for wind farms and solar arrays, but for environmentally-friendly polish and post-consumer waste clothing. I am serious about doing well by doing good. I'm a conscientious consumer, and

I think Dalton would be proud of me, wherever he is.

So, goodsmell is the last stop on my list. No really, goodsmell—one word, all lowercase, like whatever that abbreviated language was in 1984 when they kept losing letters. Or e.e. cummings' poem about the "little goat-footed balloon man." Or not.

The funny thing is that goodsmell doesn't smell like anything, at least not to me. The salesgirl, chic in a hemp Calvin Klein shift, eyes my silk jersey wrap dress with concern.

"Hi, welcome to goodsmell. This is your first time visiting our perfumery." It's a statement, not a question.

I tap the enamel V pinned to my Diane vonFurstenburg, so she will rest assured it is indeed vintage. Her face softens as she realizes silkworms were harvested in the 70's for this dress, but I haven't personally harmed any. She taps on her own O pin. Yeah, zero-carbon clothing. I'm not surprised.

"I'm Saffron. I'm here to help you find your signature scent."

She turns my wrist and spritzes it. Except there's no spit to the spritz, just a puff of air.

"I think it's empty...."

"Oh, no," Saffron coos. "That's just right. We've found that alcohol and similar bases are toxic to the environment. So, to stay green, we've captured the essence of each scent."

"It's air? Ninety-five dollars for air?"

"Not air. Essence. It's completely different. A completely different thing, a different word."

She hands me a tiny jar of coffee beans. "Okay, clear your nasal palette."

I breathe in obligingly. She puffs a series of essences on separate spots up my arms. Açai berry, bamboo, chocolate and neroli, black pepper and rosehips, amber-patchouli. I learn that the bottles are made of 100% recycled glass and aluminum. All organic, sustainable, fair trade ingredients and 5% of every purchase would go to something important in Africa. I don't smell anything. I don't feel anything.

She reaches for a bottle of green tea essence. I sing under my breath, "There is only air where I used to care."

"What's that?"

"Oh, nothing, just humming. Hey, thanks for your time, but I think I'll keep looking."

"Was that 'There is Only Air'?"

"Yeah…."

"I love that song. I haven't listened to The Owls in ages."

"Oh, well, my boyfriend likes them, liked them. My ex-boyfriend likes them." Why was I telling her this?

"Yeah, mine did, too." A moment of silence lingers between us for the might-as-well-be-departed.

"Don't leave yet," Saffron says. "I think I've got something you'll like. Just hold on a sec."

She locks the front door and dims the lights, then leads me through the Employees Only door. Okay, she's either Sapphic or a serial killer or wants to show me the latest Earthwatch video. But, I'm curious.

"Just to warn you, these cost a lot—I mean a lot—of carbon offsets."

Saffron reveals a bevy of plump bottles in jewel tones. I can smell something familiar; my sense memory is sparking.

"May I?" I hold up a burnt orange bottle, heavy with liquid.

Saffron smiles. I squeeze the atomizer bulb and I'm enveloped in the scent of chicken and dumplings combined with sweet potato pie. It's just like grandma's. The next bottle is Valvoline and Dr. Pepper, like gas stations used to smell. The next is the creamy artifice of Styrofoam. Another, the musky, pungent odor of my Mediterranean college crush. Another, cinnamon rolls melting with real butter.

"Men just can't get enough of that one," she whispers. "So, you're single, right?"

"Mm-hm."

"I have just the thing." She wraps a ruby-tinted bottle in crinkling yellow paper, placing it carefully in a bag. "Just wait to spray it 'til you're out of the store. I don't want the EPA following the trail in."

I hand her my card and sign without even reading the receipt.

"Thanks."

"Thank me after you've tried it." She flicks on the lights, and unlocks the door. "Have fun."

I duck under the gallery awning and regloss my lips. I tug my new sweater down to bare my clavicle and the tops of my shoulders. And I spray myself liberally with my signature scent.

Before I'm a foot down the pavement, men are turning their heads. They smell me and remember their most favorite days. A new note wafts with each step: toasted sesame seeds, then the tang and salt of the pickle, the rich cheese, the charcoal, and the perfect char on the hamburger itself.

I have nothing but hope.

The Shiner

A struggling young women resorts to a little con.

With a name like Ever, one would assume more permanency. At least something substantial. Not this fleeting, precarious creature. Not this mess.

For ever and ever. Instead, it was one small drama after another. Bad choices all. Or good choices squandered. Whenever there was a lucky break, a little bit of money or love, it was fleeting, and Ever ended up worse off than before.

There was poor and there was broke. And Ever prided herself on merely being broke and not belonging to an unfortunate class. She used to believe in the nobility of the poor. There was romanticism to it, almost Dickensian, as if being poor meant being good. Poor but simple. Happy in a cold-water flat, mending socks, making do. But day to day, passing by convenience stores and bus stops, and parking lots, seeing those girls hanging it all out on the fire escape of the local motel, not so much. Poor just looked sick and awful. Poor was not noble, it was trashy. And at her poorest, or most broke, Ever was determined not to let it show. She might steal the silverware, but she would use the correct fork for the correct course.

She was at the supermarket, a rarity, as it was her unspoken rule to generally eat what she did not have to pay for. The rule kept her svelte and in the company of cocktail parties, book launches, gallery shows, and the occasional sampling at the import grocer. That day, she waited behind two customers she quickly labeled as *white trash*. The man was thin, his jaw line awkward, with several teeth gone. The woman was thin, too, but lumpy in the wrong places. Her hair was truly dishwater, stringy and lank. They both wore stretched, well-laundered tee shirts which promoted events they had never attended, perhaps never heard of. The man argued with the checkout girl about the price of soda. He was skeptical about the price, the scanner, the state of the economy. It was just one more way that The Man was out to get him. The checkout girl smiled weakly. The soda was already on special: buy one case, get two free. There is only so low you can go. The woman pushed a limp lock of hair behind her ear and asked if the carts were the kind that could go off the premises. The checkout girl did not understand.

"Can these leave the pre-mi-seees?" the woman repeated, gesturing to the shopping cart. "Or are they the kind whose wheels all lock up when you take them past the yellow line?"

The checkout girl just smiled again, as if she was dealing with a foreign exchange student.

The woman, mildly frustrated, turned to the man and asked if they could take the bus.

"The bus?" he laughed. And with that laugh she knew,

anybody in the supermarket knew, there was no way he was spending money on transit. They were walking. They were walking with three cases of soda, no cart, no bus. Ever felt awful for this woman. This woman looked fifty but was probably closer to thirty-five. The one thing she could look forward to was taking a grocery cart of the premises and not be required to lug all those cans home. And you could tell just by looking at her that she never thought of leaving the laughing man. Never could consider arguing with him or imagining there would be anyone else who would want her.

And as much as it hurt Ever's heart to see this, she was absolutely certain she was far from it. That no matter how broke she got, she would not ever be what the woman was. If not genetically predisposed, she possessed a sort of social constitution that would not let her cross that threshold into trash. Counting her own pennies out in line, she added more items to the list of things she would never do:

1. Never wear hair curlers out in public.
2. And no flip flops. Or, if so, only at the beach.
3. Never take the bus, unless it was by sense of adventure or as ironic adaptation.
4. Never wear open toe shoes unless her toenails were painted.
5. And honestly, never go out with chipped polish, fingers or toes.

6. Never chew gum.

7. Never smoke off-brand cigarettes — only Gauloises or Dunhill, and then with a slow detachment and a suitable drink.

8. And never slang. She detested the ugly lilt of it, no lightness or beauty,

The list was much longer, constantly changing as she observed the terrible business of strangers. Though she became more and more broke, no exceptions were made. Only additions of things that must not be given in or given up when the money was gone. The less resources one has to draw from, the more that appearances must be kept up. It was not always like this. Most people were very generic in the things they loved and specific in the things they abhorred. Ever, on the other hand, was tethered by many small, specific happinesses and when she disliked something, it was usually large and unable to be boxed. Perhaps it was always like this, but not as desperately, transparently so.

Ever Irene Kennedy. When things were different, she had been pictured in the social pages. The combination of a quirky first name with an old money last name got her seventy-five percent to anywhere. Charisma, impeccable charm, and the wardrobe did the rest. She sometimes wished for a plain name, one that at least conjured lower expectations. Even her wardrobe came and went as it was sold and re-bought time after time through consignment and other strange arrangements.

When she did make money, it was gone as fast as, as fast as it could be spent. As fast as those clueless boys who fell for the husk of her voice when whiskeyed, the red lipstick of a time gone by, the way she was raptly attentive when they spoke, laughed at all the right moments, at least for a little while. It worked for everybody, for a little while, and she could forget that she was lonely in the world. It was a fierce anachronism, being able to draw them in with honey but not being able to make anything stick.

Life seemed to be tougher for her than for most. There was not an ease to anything. Everything, from the cocktail to the laugh to the seam on the stocking was painfully preplanned. It was work, and she seemed to work and work just to get by.

And though she did not know it, there were many men – from the Chinese delivery guy to the to the local coffee shop boy – who longed to kiss her the way she longed to be kissed. They imaged her porcelain skin under their lips and teeth and took great time imagining the creation of a purple black bruise. They thought with great tenderness of the violent, fox-like bite they could deliver to her pale neck. They couldn't know how skittish she'd become about people and happiness. She had not yet resorted to the little con. Others with more calibrated moral compasses than she had may have already considered her to have crossed over to criminal activity. But, as her struggles usually went, she ended up being short of illegal and sort of scraped things together just enough to hurt no one but herself. All the unpaid bills just piled up in a little basket until she used the oldest of them as kindling. She stopped shredding for security of her personal information long ago, as she assumed her credit score was so damn thrashed that no one who stole her identity could gain a thing. It fact, they may well improve upon it. At any rate, she did not imagine that she could serve any time for these sorts of issues. There was no longer such a thing as debtor's prison. And, if there were, she would surely be in it and there would be no one to get her out.

It was Ever's internal meter of class and aspiration that kept her from participating in low class behavior. There was her list of preferences and her arbiters of grace – some she recognized in herself and some that were so innate to her that they could not be reasoned or separated. Once one is willing to act without sentimental detachment, moral relativism enters quickly in. At some point, she wanted to figure out if truth and right were the same. But not yet.

It was the black eyeliner that gave her the idea. Thick kohl from the gypsy store filled with random religious relics, belly-dancing outfits, and all sorts of holistic stuff that didn't do anyone any good. Where the women went to buy things to make them feel exotic and empowered, but came home to the same lonely frozen dinners.

The kohl eyeliner did not wear well on her. It bloomed around her eye like a bruise. There was no sex to it. The black she'd drawn on would go perfect with a redneck husband in an undershirt letting her know that he didn't intend on telling her twice. Ever, with no husband of her own, invented one. An imaginary husband who demanded dinner hot and filled the recycling bin with bottle glass. She wore long sleeves to cover the imaginary bruises and large sunglasses to cover the drawn-on shiner. She adopted a posture less confident than her standard deportment. No strut in the gait, no swing to the hips. She adopted a glance behind her an imaginary fear. And then she went to the local thrift store.

The shop was meant to benefit women escaping a violent environment, women and children who truly had to run for their abusers, whether married to them or strangers. The store served a dual purpose, to raise funds from its meager sales to support the safe house and counselors for the women in need, and to provide a place for the women, who had escaped oftentimes with little more than the clothes on their backs, a place to get new things to take on their hopefully safe journeys away. Ever wore her dark glasses, her long sleeves, and furtive glances to the shop. She tried on the nicest clothes it had to offer. It was amazing the things that more tony women had donated. Just a season off, but still so chic, and often valuable. Always in good repair, for each only was worn a time or two before its season ended and it was replaced by something similar in slightly different hue. Slightly up or down hem, a little more or less embellishment. Ever took an armful of clothes, mindful not to take too long or to take anything that would be considered evening wear, which would not be compatible to her imaginary state. She skulked up to the register, looked behind her and whispered, "Can you help me please? I need to go."

The woman at the register knew, or thought she knew, just by looking at her, what her situation was. She looked like every other woman who needed a safe place, though by the black eye whose edges peeked out beyond the rim of her sunglasses, her last punch was a little worse than average. They sometimes came to the store when they did not know where else to go. The location of the safe house was so secret that many of the women who really needed its services were unsure themselves how to get there if the indeed could leave their poor homes. Ever had taken a lighter hand with the kohl, using more hues of green and blue, purple and a little yellow to appropriate bruises in the various signs of healing, as if the punch were not a single incident but part of the culture of her unfortunate imaginary home.

The woman took one more look at her and quietly confided, "Is he waiting outside?"

"I don't know what you mean," Ever bluffed, secretly gratified the woman was buying her bit.

"Tap the case if he's waiting outside or you think he may have followed you."

"Maybe?" Ever hedged.

The woman putting her hand on top of Ever's, saying nothing. Ever tapped the glass once.

"Just take the clothes, dear," the woman whispered. "Just go, we'll take care of it. There's an exit for staff in the back. And you can catch a cab on Vann Ness if you need. Here's ten dollars…"

"I couldn't," protested Ever, but her voice lacked conviction.

"Go," the woman insisted. She gave Ever a large tote bag right of the rack and put the center's card. "Call the hotline when you can. We're here to help. The woman paused thoughtfully, "Just don't go back."

Ever, almost regretful that she was pulling a con on such a nice, sincere woman, almost paused. But what could she do but go through with it? It was like pulling a con on a priest. You couldn't admit it. Then, was no turning back. The best you could do was to try not to do the same thing in the future. It was Maslow's hierarchy of needs at work again. If you had to fight for food and shelter and basic security then you couldn't rally be concerned with love or friendship or any of that rot.

In that movie, the one where the gangster's moll gets lessons to smarten her up, and falls in love with the straitlaced teacher instead of her vaguely mob boss boyfriend, she talks about how much her blue-collar father thought a hot lunch was important. That if you woke up every morning and still wanted a hot cup of coffee, that if you felt that you still deserved a nice, hot lunch, than you couldn't be ready to end it all, and you didn't despair of God's mercy. There were still earthly pleasures that you desired. And, no matter how dark things were for Ever, she still wanted coffee in a china cup. Still wanted a pair of alligator shoes, and still despaired over a broken tube of lipstick, still wanted what she wanted.

There was a rosary she'd bought at the same time as the kohl, a last-minute impulse form the counter crowed with fat buddhas, incense, silver bracelets, and little saints. Even she knew that sacramentals were not sacraments, but still blessed things, and they were meant to be treated reverently. If they came to be damaged or worn out, you had to dispose of them in the correct way: either dig a hole in the ground and bury them, or set them on fire. With her bare hands, she dug a little hole in the green median in the shop's parking lot and buried the rosary.

Oh, she was ever so sorry. And, she ever so was.

Temporary Insanity

An office romance becomes uncomfortably complicated.

Bisbee's bottom itched hot with carpet burns, and her shoulder was scratched pink, courtesy of the keyboard tray. She was happily rife with bruises and bites and, in fact, dressed more conservatively now than before the misadventures began, lest she spike the curiosity of Human Resources. But her flushed cheeks and steam-curled hair, golden-red like the copper town for which she was named, were hard to hide.

Things started innocently enough. They were just two misplaced journalists who the unfortunate job market had driven corporate. After too many days of compartmentalized copywriting, Bisbee wrote a fabulous, and not repeatable, filthy joke on Babbitt's proofing sheet. This led to a flurry of dirty little post-it notes. Sexy suggestions of things only English majors would to each other, with footnotes on how positions may vary according to AP or Chicago style.

Soon those long grey days were broken by stolen moments before and after, and a few times during, office hours. Bisbee lived for the pressure of the water cooler against the small of her back, the white tap releasing a stream down her thigh. The acrid taste of company coffee on his mouth. The department-morale meetings during which she slipped off her shoe under the conference table, trying to keep poker-faced as her bare toes worked up his chair.

It wasn't just last night under her desk—or the elevator,

bathroom stall, or electrical room. She knew Babbitt had true affection. He brought a mirror to entertain her lonely Beta fish, Blue. Among salacious text messages, there were sweet ones like *you're the bee's knees*. And, he took a light hand editing her, writing *please* and *sorry* in the margins.

The best was yet to come. The two were booked for a copy editing conference in Vegas. Bisbee dreamed of the desert and its neon signs bright with electric sex. She craved nights that went long past five, free cocktails to lower her few last inhibitions, and finally getting to use a bed.

Tuesday, over Vietnamese takeout, Babbitt confided, "I called the hotel and made arrangements for adjoining rooms…"

Bisbee was so excited she stabbed him with a plastic fork. The tines broke against his khaki-clad muscled thigh, but she still kissed the spot in apology later.

Though Bisbee generally kept a blank and unsentimental workspace, the navy envelope containing her plane ticket was T-pinned lovingly right above the fishbowl. It was a company function, after all, and Bisbee was a valued employee. Her manager even hired a temp to cover the workload during her absence. Bisbee had two days to train her. From day one, they were enemies. Her name was Iskra or Ilonka or something else foreign. Bisbee refused to learn it, really because the temp was younger, prettier, and skinnier. Every seat swiveled when the temp walked past. She received several invitations to Friday's potluck, cajoled that she didn't even have to bring anything.

The temp leaned forward to ask something, and her skirt hitched up showing a slice of black garter. It reminded Bisbee of the stockings she purchased specially for the hotel, and it made her green that she wasn't the type to wear them every day. Bisbee took in the temp's cat-shaped eyes, full bottom lip, breasts high and tight under a v-neck. She blew off the request to borrow her style guide.

"And don't feed my fish while I'm gone," Bisbee warned.

The next day, she resolved friendliness. It was Bisbee and Babbitt who were going to Vegas after all, and envy was so unbecoming. She came in at 7:46, hoping to rendezvous between the reams of white and canary yellow. She was pleased to see steaming coffee on Babbitt's desk.

Bisbee tried the door to the copy room, but it wouldn't budge. She could hear the whine of the archaic printer warming up. Several thumps followed. She knocked.

"Babbitt?" she whispered. "Hey, Babbitt-Rabbit, are you in there?" The door was still locked.

Returning to her cubicle, Bisbee shifted from confusion to panic. A fresh cup of coffee sat on the temp's desk, too.

Bisbee did the only thing she knew to do in times of crisis. She cleaned. She pulled the guts out of the latest edition of Webster's, and put it and every other living bit of paper in the confidential shredding bin. She tossed her mug and fern. She carried Blue over to the coffee island and turned on the tap. The hapless Beta slid into the drain, and Bisbee pulsed the disposal. She was wiping down her desk when the temp resurfaced. The girl adjusted her skirt and smiled.

"Hey, what happened to your fish?"

"He died." Bisbee betrayed no emotion. They both looked at the empty spot where the little bowl once sat.

"But where's my ticket?" Bisbee spat at the temp. "It was right here!"

"What ticket?"

"Oh come on," shouted Bisbee. "You been here 24 hours and you've christened the copy machine and taken my trip to Vegas!"

Bisbee reached over the divider and pulled the girl's shiny

black hair—hard. The temp shrieked. Babbitt ran down the aisle.

"What the hell…?"

"My ticket," she repeated.

"Oh for God's sake," said Babbitt, "I have it right here. I was just checking seat assignments to see if we were together." He regarded the empty cubicle and shook his head. "We are."

Bisbee regarded Babbitt. He had left his pen uncapped and red stain bloomed on his pocket. He looked like any and every other guy in the office in a blue oxford and khakis. She surveyed the grey-blue maze of cubicles, took the navy envelope, tore off the top ticket, and left.

There are better boxes to be had. An airplane seat, a lavatory, a hotel room, each square self-contained. There is a place for every tiny coffeepot and cup, a precision and beauty to the arrangement of single-serving soap. And there are banks of slot machines, endless glistening rows making up bright new cubicle farms.

Author's Notes

Gentle Reader,

First, thank you for taking a chance on me. There are millions of books circulating unread all over the world, and I appreciate that you were curious enough about *Secret Breakfast* to crack the cover. The stories are short – between 500 and 2,500 words – and plentiful, so even if you don't like one, you may like another. And if you don't like any, that may be the storyteller's fault, not yours. This sad fact explains why writers toil and drink in solitude and growing misanthropy.

And while I don't wear black every single day or chain smoke or other such writerly pursuits, I was inspired to write a book of stories on loneliness, isolation, and redemption. The truth is that I didn't intend to write a book about fresh starts, second helpings, and great escapes, but that I found these consistent themes across almost all of my stories. There is a tinge of melancholy in the premise. However, there is the shimmering hope that, regardless of circumstance, there is the possibility of a new life.

Each story in *Secret Breakfast* approaches the theme of escape in a few small pages. I absolutely adore short fiction, especially the stories of Dorothy Parker, O. Henry, F. Scott Fitzgerald, and Flannery O'Connor. I appreciate the fierce economy of words and the challenge of telling a complete story in a very small space. Some of my stories were written for competition, and some for challenges of my own design. Most have three elements vying for the same little space: the practical matters (word count, genre, location, object); the inspiration (a poem, piece of music, etc.); and the theme.

I'd like to share my thoughts about a few of the stories in *Secret Breakfast*. If you've gotten this far, I don't believe I will spoil the endings. (However, if you ever are in a quandary about whether or not a character is dead, has died, or was murdered, the answer is probably *yes*.)

This brings me to "The Changing Room." I was tasked to write a suspense involving a locker in less than 2,500 words. I have always been fascinated with class, society, and culture in America. I wanted to write a young woman's version of *The Talented Mr. Ripley*, with nods to that author in the name of the resort. This is also the story where I really began to have fun with names (see Brewster and the coffee beans). "The Changing Room" is the piece which helped me realize that I was happiest and best within the confines of the short, short story.

Curiously, "The Gulf of Aden" has a soft spot in my heart. I think of it as "The Pirate Story," which would have perhaps been a better name. The logistics – a drama located on a cruise ship – were quite different than "The Changing Room," but I was again inspired to write about division of wealth. This time, though, when the social-climber gets what she thought she wanted, it's really not that wonderful at all. I had read a newspaper article about the precautions some cruise lines were taking when sailing through the Gulf of Aden, and I wondered what would happen if they didn't take any.

A news account was also the inspiration for "Buses and Planes." I was given the task of writing a horror story that took place at a bus stop. I had read accounts of the Lindbergh kidnapping and pursued a historical fiction-fantasy approach to the fate of the perpetrator. Around the same time, I'd read a news story about convalescent homes in Germany that had erected fake bus shelters to give the elderly a place to burn their nervous energy. The characters and the details of the Lindbergh affair are true, but I've just imagined a different fate.

Similarly, "Cold Call" was inspired by aviatrix Beryl Markham. When I received the challenge of writing a ghost story about a salesman or saleswoman, the pink polyester-clad cosmetician came right to mind. She seemed so different from the Beryl I'd been reading about; it was fun to put them together. But, I didn't really know what would happen until I researched the other meanings of the word "beryl." The mineral definition helped me decide what would happen next.

A name can set the course for the story. In "Temporary Insanity," a drama in less than 1,000 words which necessitated a cubicle location and the inclusion of a plane ticket, all of the names are wild. I've named Bisbee for Sam Bisbee who sings "Cubicle Love Song," though the story indicates a different provenance. Babbit, of course, is named for the ultimate conformist from the eponymous book.

The strangest perimeters are that of "ScentEasy": a political satire, set in a perfume shop, and including a hamburger... in less than 1,000 words. I'm quite proud of that one. And, I was pleasantly surprised to win the Environmental Futures Writing Prize for it. Good stories, regardless of genre, tell us about our relationships with each other and our connection, or disconnection, with the natural world. So, modestly, I think this does that.

"Phoning Arcadia," another flash fiction piece, is a bit tender, too. The challenge was to write a romantic comedy set in an arcade of some sort and to include a coffee pot. My inspiration was Edward Hopper's 1927 painting of the Automat. The woman's hat and coat are of two different seasons, but you know they're the best she's got as she looks into that lonely coffee cup.

A lesser-known painting inspired "My Better Nature." Minnesota painter Scott Lloyd Anderson's "Boathouse, Lake Calhoun, Minneapolis" provided a picture of the silent overturned vessels ribbed with snow. The challenge was to write a horror story located in the trunk of a car, and to also include a candle. "My Better Nature," "Delicates," and "Written on the Skin" are all from a male first-person point-of view. My version of what men may think, or horror for that matter, may not be as gritty as others, but I enjoy writing across genres while still staying true to my literary style.

There are a good number of first-person stories from a woman's perspective and third-person stories that sympathize with one. But, there are also stories that follow a silverfish ("The Voracious Reader") and an automobile ("Cleanliness Is"). "Duck, Duck, Goose" is told in the second-person/imperative voice. And, "Fruit of the Spirit" is told in the first-person plural. I had wanted to write in the "we" voice – as a group that shared the same point of view. The unnamed sisters in "Fruit of the Spirit" react together to their saintly new neighbors. In this story, I was able to write about one of my favorite things – eating. You'll find food running through the book: from the endless chicken in "Flightless Birds" to the buffet in The Gulf of Aden" to the forbidden charcuterie in "The Cleaver" to the scents in "ScentEasy".

And, drink, of course. As noted in "Lonely Exile," it can be a comfort and a curse. The cocktail, in one form or another, appears across classes in many of the tales. "Absinthe Minded" is a lighter take on it, written to satisfy a science fiction/police station/ruler challenge. I won't wax on any more about it here. It's late and coffee would be the prudent option.

It seems the *Secret Breakfast* stories are cocktails in and of themselves: a dash of bitters, some simple sugar, and at their best, hopefully, intoxicating. There's so much beauty in the world: chickens and eggs, bees and honey, party dresses, the sound of trains, riots of color in spring, and the promise a new suitcase holds. I have tried to capture a little piece of it in each story, even the ones that break my heart. I have so much more to tell you about it all. I hope I have written something you would like to read, and left out the parts which you would not. And, I most hope that I've written the kind of stories that you can read again and again.

~ Candace Leigh Coulombe

Questions for Discussion

1. The stories range from a little more than 500 words to a little less than 2,500. As a reader, is your experience changed by the length of the story? How successful was the author at telling a complete story in a few pages?

2. The stories are divided into two categories: Fantastic and Domestic. For the pieces in the Fantastic section, what elements are outside of the natural realm? Do spiritual, supernatural, or mystic elements impact your engagement in the story of empathy with the characters? Do you prefer one category over another? And, are there any "domestic" stories which you believe are "fantastical," or the other-way-round?

3. The stories "Fruit of the Spirit," "Cleanliness Is," and "Intercession" have a distinctly Catholic influence. "The Still-Sleeping World" and "The Cleaver" have Judaic themes. Was the author able to maintain reverence for the religion when the stories had fantastical elements? In what other stories does the author address the concepts of faith, grace, or divine intervention?

4. The author says that "a name can set a course for the story." In addition to Highsmith Resort, Bisbee, Babbit, and Beryl, what names of characters, places, and objects are imbued with deeper meaning?

5. Color plays a role in many of the stories. In "Cold Call" pinks and greens are prominent. How is the color green used in other stories? What other colors are tied to narrative?

6. Food also plays a role in the stories. Consider the symbolism of food or drink in the pieces. How did what was being eaten or imbibed reflect each character's state – of mind, class, or romantic prospects?

7. The author says that she is influenced by class and division of wealth. Compare and contrast the lead characters in "The Changing Room," "The Shiner," and "The Gulf of Aden." What other stories are driven by, or touch on, class discrepancies and aspirations?

8. Many of the pieces refer to other authors, books, and poems. "Lonely Exile" notes the influence of Keats; and "The Voracious Reader" is steeped in hard-boiled classics. What other literary references have you found in the book? Is it necessary to be familiar with the literature mentioned to appreciate its relevance to the story? If you were to write a story based on your favorite poem – from childhood or now – what would it be?

9. Loneliness and isolation are central to these stories. In which stories are the characters running towards solitude, and in which are they running away from it? Not every lonely ache is romantic in nature. What other types of wants do the characters have? It has been said that "isolation is the harshest form of poverty." Do you agree?

10. As in the collection *Second Grace*, the stories in *Secret Breakfast* address opportunities for a fresh start. The characters can go, stay, or change. If a character changes, is it by choice or by circumstance? If not, what does "stay" mean in the context of the story?

**See the indicated page if you wish
to read a story about...**

**Or, if you wish
to read a story about...**

About the Author

Fabulist Candace Leigh Coulombe lives and writes in Northern California with her husband and three young children. She works as a full-time corporate marketing communications specialist and a part-time writer of flash fiction, fables, and amusements.

To learn more about Coulombe's work or the fables collected in *Secret Breakfast*, please visit **www.secretbreakfast.com** or follow **@eggandink**.

Made in the USA
Charleston, SC
16 April 2013